SILENT Knight

BETH BOLDEN

1. Ice Rink
2. Dancing Sugar Plums
3. Santa's Workshop
4. Frosty's
5. Nutcrackers
6. Tidings & Joy
7. Gingerbread Cottage
8. Ginger's Breads
9. The White Elephant
10. The Snowflake Shack
11. Jolly Java
12. Season's Readings
13. Mistletoe Movies
14. Rudolph's
15. Christmas Falls Festivals Inc
16. Festival Museum

CHAPTER 1

JEREMIAH KNIGHT, BETTER KNOWN to his friends and fellow teammates as Jem, wished he was anywhere but where he actually was—back in Christmas Falls, the small town he'd grown up in, and *left* as soon as he was able.

But here he was. Back in Christmas Falls, with its quaint streets festooned with strands of lights and Christmas trees on every single block and utterly pervasive sense of holiday cheer.

It was not only that he was back, Jem considered as he leaned back in his chair at Frosty's, the local bar. It was that he was back *and* every eye was on him.

What had possessed him to say yes to the honorary grand marshal position after the festival council had come calling?

Don't be stupid. You know exactly why.

Yes, he'd been feeling pretty goddamn sorry for himself right around then, recovering from a season-ending pectoral injury, not sure if he'd ever play again, and definitely not alongside his best friend.

Deacon, Jem thought, as he scratched at the wooden coaster with a thumbnail, believed he was so good at keeping secrets but he was utter shit at it. Jem had known, maybe even before Deacon did, that he'd be retiring at the end of the season.

Why else convince Jem to come back and play one more year for the Charleston Condors, the football team they'd both loved being a part of?

Now, that rosy future where they redeemed the Condors' reputation and went to the playoffs and ended their careers on a high note, *together*, was done. Finished. Destroyed.

Jem wouldn't be playing, and then Deacon was going to retire.

Was it any wonder that he'd not just hung right up on the festival committee when they'd called?

He'd been, as his mother liked to say, *wallowing*.

Well, he was never going to goddamn wallow again, if *this* was the end result.

He was stuck in Christmas Falls from Thanksgiving until New Year's.

Normally, he'd pop in for a day or two, see his parents, then leave.

But not this year.

One day down, forty-five to go.

"Looking awfully glum there," the guy behind the bar said. Jem knew him. Recognized him. Wasn't that Mik, who'd been a few years behind him? Played hockey. He was *pretty* sure it was Mik.

Jem wanted to tell the guy that he *felt* kind of glum. But nobody wanted a bummed-out guy at the head of the parade, or at any of the events the email he'd gotten a week ago had outlined.

He was supposed to be the "guardian of Christmas cheer" or so the email had stated.

The problem was that he'd never felt less cheerful in his whole fucking life.

So he just shrugged and tapped his beer glass.

Thankfully, Mik got the message that he wasn't particularly interested in talking and *definitely* not interested in talking about his sour mood and walked off to pull him another pint.

"What's there to be so glum about?" a voice next to him asked.

He glanced over as a guy with a thick dark beard and equally dark eyes slid onto the barstool next to him.

The man was dressed in a plaid shirt, pulled tight across his broad shoulders, jeans and boots. And there was something undeniably familiar about him.

Or maybe it wasn't familiarity but instead, attraction.

Because Jem felt it zing right up his spine as their eyes met.

"Nothing," Jem said, forcing himself to smile in a friendly way.

It wasn't as hard to fake cheer with this guy as it had been with Mik. Jem didn't need a diagram to explain exactly why that was.

"No? It was someone else frowning into his beer then." The guy grinned, and there it was again—that undeniable flutter at the base of his stomach. "My mistake."

"I just…" Jem cleared his throat. He *had* been sitting here and sulking.

Not just tonight, a voice inside his head chimed in. *But for way too many nights recently.*

Maybe he could do something about that.

A little light flirtation could hardly help but boost his spirits. And this guy seemed like a prime candidate. Jem was hardly a small guy—after all, he'd been a linebacker in the NFL, was *still* a linebacker in the NFL he reminded himself—but the man next to him had at least a few inches on him and even wider shoulders under all that plaid.

Was he a lumberjack for a living?

Not a fantasy Jem had ever thought he'd have, but it turned out it was undeniably appealing.

"You just?" He raised an eyebrow.

"Didn't ever expect that I'd be sitting here back at Frosty's," Jem said. Could hear Deacon poking him in the back of his brain, telling him to *do better*. And he could, surely. People were always telling him he was charming, even though it felt like he'd expended very little effort to earn that adjective.

"Back at Frosty's? Seems to me that it'd be hard to miss you. If you'd showed up before, I sure would've noticed."

"Yeah?"

The guy shot him a look. "Um, *yeah*."

"Oh."

He nudged Jem in the side. "You're kind of...conspicuous."

Said the mountain of a man clad in an ocean of plaid with the twinkly eyes and the bright smile.

But then, *yes*, Jem understood what the guy was saying. Jem was an NFL player and a hometown hero, as much as he'd wanted to avoid being painted with that particular brush. While he might not be easily recognizable in his day-to-day life, here in Christmas Falls, it was probably inevitable that he'd be spotted.

Jem told himself that he wasn't disappointed at all that the guy had come over because he'd recognized him—not because he'd actually *wanted* to.

"Right," Jem said flatly. "You want an autograph?"

The guy's jaw dropped. "Is that why…" But instead of asking the question, he shook his head emphatically. "No," he said. "No, that's not why I wanted to talk to you."

"Oh. Good." Jem smiled. Relieved in a way that surprised him. He didn't even know this guy's name.

"I meant it, you know," he said, "you can tell me about it if you want."

"Tell you about it?"

"Why you were frowning into your beer."

"Oh. Well." Jem hesitated. He didn't like talking about it. Not with anyone. Especially not a stranger, even a stranger with those shoulders and those eyes. Even when he wondered if his beard would feel soft against his skin or prickly. "I just thought I'd be back in Charleston right now. Playing in a game tomorrow. Not sitting here, nursing a beer, wondering what the fuck I'm going to do with my life."

That was way more honesty than he'd intended to lay out, but once it was out of his mouth, Jem didn't want to immediately snatch it back.

Maybe it was the empathy in the guy's dark eyes. *Empathy* not sympathy. Sympathy made Jem want to clear off the bar with one massive swipe of his arm. But what he was seeing wasn't that at all.

"Ah," Sexy Lumberjack said. "Yeah, I saw you got hurt a few weeks back. That really fucking sucks."

"Yeah." An understatement of the year. Of the *century*.

"There's no hope you can still play this year?"

Jem's gaze must've narrowed because the guy threw his head back, laughing. "No, no, I'm not a scout for an opposing team, I promise. Just...we'll say a concerned citizen."

"Are you?"

"A citizen?"

Jem nodded.

"Yeah." Sexy Lumberjack shot him an odd look. "Of course I am. I grew up here. Same as you."

"We know each other, then." Jem had wondered. There had been that split second of familiarity before it had faded into something else entirely.

"Of course we do." Sexy Lumberjack paused. "You really don't recognize me, do you?"

Jem scrambled, his brain whirling through his high school graduating class. But none of those guys had worn a beard like this or been built like a monster truck.

Of course, back when he'd been eighteen, he hadn't looked like he did now, either.

He'd been pimply, too-tall, gangly, with not nearly enough weight on his bones.

But nobody he could remember matched this guy's face.

"You don't." The guy answered before Jem could. But instead of sounding insulted, he sounded amused. "You really don't."

"Sorry," Jem said, reluctantly shaking his head.

"No, it's...it's funny, is what it is."

Jem would've said it was something else.

"So, no hope of playing this year?" the guy asked before Jem could give in and ask him what his name was.

"Uh, no. Not really." The pectoral tear had been severe, and he'd needed surgery to repair it. Even with all the excellent medical care and rehab he was getting from the Condors, the best the doctors could promise was February or March.

Too late for him to rejoin the team for this season.

Too late for him to rejoin Deacon before his best friend hung his cleats up for good.

"That really sucks. I'm sorry." The man's touch on his arm was fleeting, but it lit up Jem's nerves, all the way to his shoulder.

"Yeah, it's not a great time."

"So that's why you came home."

Was Christmas Falls home? Jem didn't really think so, not anymore. Certainly, he'd never believed that was true when he'd been growing up, when he'd been wild to leave. But then Charleston didn't feel like home, either, not anymore.

Not when he was no longer part of the Condors' season.

"Yeah," Jem said, because it was easier to agree, than to continue talking—or *thinking*—about how it felt like he no longer belonged any fucking where.

The guy nudged him again. "Well, we're glad to have you back."

Would they be so happy if they knew how reluctant Jem was about coming back?

You know how to do this, Deacon-in-his-brain reminded him. *Change the subject. Flirt with the guy. You want to. And God knows you're capable of it.*

"We know *all* about me, apparently, but what about you?"

"What about me?" The guy's eyebrows rose. They were the same gorgeous dark mink color as the beard, and just as soft looking.

Jesus, Jem wanted the guy to rub his face all over his naked body.

Hold up. Deacon chimed in. *You're just flirtin' with him. That's all. You don't need any more reasons to be conflicted about this fucking place.*

Amen to that.

"What do you do?" Jem asked, taking a sip of his beer. He motioned to Mik to bring the other guy a refill of his own.

"You really want to know?"

"Well, *yeah,*" Jem said. He grinned. "How else am I supposed to flirt with you?"

He'd said it, partly because *one*, it was true. And *two*, because he'd gotten the vibe this guy wouldn't be averse to some flirtation, but it was impossible to say for sure. So he'd decided to make his interest blatantly obvious.

"Oh. Oh. Well. Um." The guy stuttered a bit, losing the confidence he'd worn like his plaid shirt for their whole conversation. "I carve stuff. Gnomes. Actually. Specifically."

"Gnomes? You carve gnomes?" That was not the answer Jem had expected him to give. But then, was anything normal in this town? Not really.

Gnome carving was such a fucking Christmas Falls profession it should've turned Jem off, but a delicious pink-ish flush crept up the guy's cheeks, and Jem decided gnome carving was actually pretty damn adorable.

Or maybe it was just the man who carved them.

"Yes," the guy said with dignity. "And other things too, but you know how it is here, Christmas is…"

"The biggest deal on the whole planet? Yeah. I know. So gnome carving it is."

"Yep."

"So, what you're really saying…" Jem paused for dramatic effect. Deacon would be so proud. "Is that you're very good with your hands."

The man choked in his beer. "Uh, yeah. *Yeah*. Oh my god."

"Oh my god?" That was not normally the reaction when Jem flirted with someone. Maybe he was worse at this than in-his-brain Deacon kept assuming he was.

"You're just..." The guy stammered again. "You're really, actually hitting on me."

"Well, *yeah*," Jem said. And this time Jem nudged him.

But when he continued to stare at Jem like he had sharpie all over his face, Jem had to add, "Is that not okay? I can stop if it makes you uncomfortable."

"No, no, *no*," the guy said. "I just...I didn't expect..."

"Trust me, I eat and shit just as much as the next person." Jem realized a second too late what he'd just said. Imaginary Deacon was now sitting on his shoulder, shaking his head.

"Goddamn it," Jem said. "I didn't mean it to come out like that."

"No, actually, it helps that you're not so great at this." The guy grinned.

"That's not usually what people say."

"I know, but I'm not most people. Not even close. I'm just..." The guy trailed off. And Jem realized then that he didn't *want* to tell Jem who he was. That he was avoiding doing it. But he *had* liked Jem hitting on him.

To say Jem was confused was an understatement.

"You're just?" Jem asked.

"Flattered."

That was not what he'd been about to say, Jem was sure of it.

"But you're not going to tell me your name. You'll tell me all about your gnomes and your hands, but not your name," Jem guessed.

"I think it was *you* saying the stuff about my hands." The guy flushed again.

It was so cute, Jem wanted to eat him alive, even *if* the guy looked like he could easily pin Jem to the wall and devour him instead.

"Fair," Jem said. "Hey! You did it again."

"Did what?" the guy asked innocently.

"Changed the subject."

"I just…" He squirmed. "I'm not sure you'd keep at this if you knew who I was."

None of that made any sense to Jem. While he'd been more than ready to leave this town, he'd liked everyone he'd gone to school with. He'd had no enemies at all. Nobody who might want to avoid him.

But then this guy didn't exactly seem like the villain in Jem's story. After all, he'd come over when he thought Jem was sad. He'd wanted to cheer him up and had offered to listen to his troubles. Someone who disliked him wouldn't have even been tempted to do that.

"I'm sure I would," Jem said softly. "Highlight of my week, so far, flirting with you."

"Wow. Okay." The guy grinned.

"I think all that's worth your name, don't you think?" Jem plastered on his most persuasive smile.

"Hmmm, maybe? You could always guess what it is..."

He could. Jem could go through every single guy he could remember from his graduating class. But that wasn't what he wanted to do.

"What about..." Jem grinned. "Nesbit?"

The guy's eyebrows skated halfway up his forehead. "Nesbit?"

"Or what about Rudyard?"

"Have you ever met anyone named Rudyard?"

Jem thought about this for a second. "Maybe you're the first?"

"Nope." He shook his head.

"Hercules?"

"Really?"

"Hey, you're built like it," Jem said, clearing his suddenly dry throat. Because *damn*, he was. And Jem had spent the last fifteen years of his life around guys who were *paid* to look this good.

"Thanks?" He blushed again. Like he could barely believe Jem was looking at him with that admiration in his eyes.

"Hey, your name could be *Jeremiah*. Is it any wonder I ended up using a nickname?"

"I think it's cute," the guy said softly. Like he actually believed that.

He might be the only person on earth besides his mother who liked that he was called Jeremiah.

"What about Ebenezer?" Jem suggested.

An eyebrow went up again. "Like Scrooge? I don't think that's me. Remember, I live here *and* I carve gnomes for a living."

"Right. Right. That's probably *me*. I'm probably Ebenezer."

The guy didn't say anything, just looked at Jem, and *God*, he probably was.

Why on earth had the committee and Griff asked him to be the "guardian of cheer" when he was so clearly the problem?

"Shit," Jem said.

"You're gonna be just fine," the guy said, patting him on the arm, but then instead of leaning in, like Jem wanted him to do, he leaned back. Finished his beer. And then before Jem could hold up his hand to ask Mik for another round, he shook his head and then stood.

"I gotta go, actually. I get up real early."

"It's..." Jem glanced at his watch. "Just after nine PM? On a Saturday night?"

But right, this was Christmas Falls. The most PG-rated town in the world. There was no nightlife to speak of, at least none that didn't involve trees and lights and candy canes and unlimited hot chocolate and, well...*gnomes.*

"I do have to get up early." He at least sounded regretful.

But not as regretful as Jem felt.

"Before I even figure out who you are?" Jem asked.

"Suppose you'll have to keep guessing," he teased.

"I'll get it right," Jem promised.

"Sure you will."

"I'll see you around?" Jem said. Wanting to grab him back, but he didn't.

Why the fuck not, Deacon-on-his-shoulder demanded.

"Oh, I'm sure you will," the guy said, and before Jem could stop him, he melted away into the crowd and the door shut behind him.

"See you've rekindled your friendship with Murphy Clark," Mik said as he gathered up the empty glass and the damp coaster.

Jem nearly fell off his barstool. "Murphy Clark?"

"Yep." Mik shot him a look, like he was stupid.

And maybe Jem was, because that couldn't have been *Murphy.*

Except...hadn't he felt familiar when Jem had first sat down?

And Murphy, Murphy who he'd been best friends with all through elementary school and junior high, had definitely had hair that dark and eyes that twinkled, even though they were so deep brown Jem had always felt like he could get lost in them.

Could he have grown up that big and tall and handsome?

Jem couldn't deny it was *possible*.

Or that he hadn't secretly thought about him, more than a handful of times, even after their friendship had cooled and they'd grown to be distant barely-acquaintances.

"I...I guess I did rekindle my friendship with Murph," Jem had to admit. Even though the truth was a lot pricklier than that, because they hadn't been flirting like friends. He couldn't deny he'd wanted something else from the guy in the plaid shirt as they'd sat talking.

But why hadn't Murphy told him? Why hadn't Murphy said who he was?

Did he think Jem wouldn't have been totally thrilled to see him again?

Sure, they'd grown apart in high school, which, at first, had upset and baffled Jem, but then he'd been too busy playing three sports, including football seriously, with an eye to a scholarship and getting the hell out of Christmas Falls, to worry about a friendship that had faded.

But he'd *never* thought that Murphy might be angry with him. Or not *want* them to be friends anymore. Murphy had always been a quiet, somewhat introspective guy. He hadn't been built like a lumberjack in high school, not like he was now, but even then he had no interest in playing sports. He'd loved art class and wood shop. He'd always been creating something, even back in elementary school when all he'd had was twigs and Elmer's glue.

Kids, Jem had realized later, long after he'd graduated and left Christmas Falls, didn't take too kindly to anyone who was different, and Murphy had always been different. He'd wished, so long after the fact it didn't make a damn bit of difference, that he'd made more of an effort to make it clear to his friend that he *liked* Murphy's kind of different.

But he hadn't.

Maybe Murphy blamed him for that, even now. He'd made sure nobody had ever bullied Murphy, but certainly he hadn't been the most popular kid in school.

You, Jem could imagine Murphy saying now, *you were the most popular kid in school.*

Yes, he probably had been. He'd been athletic and going places. He'd been laid-back and unconcerned about charming anyone, which it turned out meant he charmed *everyone*.

He certainly hadn't looked for popularity, but it had found him anyway, and yes, he could acknowledge now, that had probably been the death knell for his early friendship with Murphy.

But he hadn't *meant* any of it.

Of course, that didn't mean Murphy didn't hold it against him, even now, all these years later.

"How's he been doing?" Jem asked Mik.

He didn't even want to think how embarrassing it was that he'd recognized Mik, who he'd only known by his reputation on the ice, and hadn't recognized Murphy, who'd been his *best friend*.

Mik raised a brow. "Murphy?"

"Yeah," Jem said, a little bit ashamed that he had to ask him. That he hadn't known himself.

They'd been inseparable for the first fifteen years of their lives.

He *should* know.

"He's doing damn good for himself," Mik said staunchly. Like he was defending Murphy, which Jem hadn't intended at all. "We love him here."

"Now that he..." God, Jem could barely say it with a straight face. "Carves gnomes for a living."

Mik leaned over the bar top. "Yeah," he said earnestly. "They're damn good gnomes. People love them. Order them online and everything. He sells out every single year."

"Really?"

Mik shot him a look. "You don't like gnomes?"

This sounded like one of those trick questions where the answer got him into serious trouble.

"No, no," Jem said quickly, "I freaking love gnomes. Gnomes are the best."

"Damn straight," Mik said before walking away toward the other end of the bar.

Chapter 2

Murphy sat back and examined the piece he'd been working on for the last few hours. He'd hoped to finish it today, but instead of calling it good, even great, he'd been nit-picking all his work.

He liked the look of it, but the truth was, he *hadn't* come home and slept well.

He'd tossed and turned, intrigued and more than a little aroused by his conversation with Jem.

Why hadn't he just told Jem who he was?

Maybe it was because Jem hadn't recognized him.

Maybe because it had felt *good* to not be Murphy in relation to Jem, for the first time.

He could be someone else—someone else that Jem might actually be interested in.

The thought had kept him up most of the night.

And this morning, had burned in the back of his brain. Instead of falling into his work, like he normally did, especially when a piece was this close to being done, he'd struggled to focus.

Still, he wasn't unhappy with the way the gnome had turned out.

Even if it felt like all the little adjustments he'd made to the face had somehow made it look just like Jem.

Whoops.

"Hey, you around?"

Murphy looked up as Griff, the organizer for the annual Christmas Falls festival, walked into his shop.

"What's up?" Murphy said, glancing over at the older man. "Is there some kind of cocoa emergency? Did we run out of Christmas lights?"

Griff made a face. "Very funny," he said. But usually that was the only reason Murphy saw the guy—when something went wrong, and Griff needed a hand.

Which Murphy was always happy to lend, if he had the time.

"Nothing's wrong," Griff continued gruffly. "Just...you know Jem Knight, right?"

"The whole town knows Jem Knight," Murphy said steadily.

He didn't want to go into details about how they'd been friends, and then they hadn't been.

"But you two were close," Griff persisted.

"Yeah, a long time ago." His words were a good reminder for both of them that those days were long over.

Griff sighed.

"You're not here because you want to add another gnome to your collection, are you?" Murphy finally asked.

"I need someone to liaise with Jem. I was thinking I'd do it myself, but it's too much with all the rest of the festival. I need to be more flexible than that—potentially in too many places at once. And Marlene mentioned that you and Jem used to be friends, plus, you know, you're always at a loose end during festival season."

It was true. By the time November rolled around, he was usually done with the gnomes he wanted to create for the year. This year was no exception. His booth at the arts and crafts fair would be stocked, and he had plenty in reserve.

He wouldn't say he was at a *loose* end, because he could always make more. They sold out, no matter how many he made, but Tasha, his single employee, kept telling him the last thing he needed was to carve a gnome for every single person who wanted one.

Scarcity economics, she'd always say to him, and he'd shake his head.

He wasn't a businessman. He just liked carving gnomes.

"Well, *yeah*, that's technically true..."

"All you'd have to do," Griff said as Murphy trailed off, unsure how he was going to dissuade the older man from this idea, "is go to the events Jem is going to. I can email you a list. And let's be honest, you'd probably be at them, anyway."

"That's it? Just be there?" *Surely, you can be in the same vicinity as Jem Knight. You did it last night.*

"Be there *with* him," Griff said.

Murphy's heart rate accelerated. "I'm not going to be *with* him," Murphy clarified with a bit of a stutter.

Griff shot him a confused look. "I mean, be around him, and make sure he has everything he needs, that he's comfortable, that he's taken care of. Possibly be his transportation, since I know parking can be tricky for some of the events."

Murphy squirmed, uncomfortable with the direction this conversation was heading. "It sounds like you want me to be his *date*."

Griff raised his eyebrows. "It does?"

"Okay, maybe not *date* but..."

"I want you to be his liaison with *me*, since I haven't mastered the technique of being in three places at once," Griff interrupted with a firm tone. "That's all. I'm an organizer, not a matchmaker."

"Right, right," Murphy said weakly.

God, this was so awkward, and he'd really put his foot in it.

Maybe Griff would take that as evidence why he'd be a terrible liaison.

But as Griff stood there, expectantly waiting for an answer—for a *yes*, because this was Griff—it was clear he didn't think that at all.

He actually wanted Murphy to do this. Introversion, poor social chatter and all.

"We're not really friends anymore," Murphy tried again.

"And there's no time like the present to rekindle that friendship," Griff retorted.

Murphy leaned back against his worktable. "You really mean all of this. You want me to do this."

"Trust me, I have plenty of crap I could be doing," Griff said. "I didn't drive out here for shits and giggles."

"Right." Murphy hesitated again. He and Griff were friendly, but he wouldn't call them *friends*. And even he knew you didn't word vomit all about ancient history onto someone who wasn't a friend.

"You wanna talk about it?" Griff asked. He glanced over at the gnome he'd been working on. "Or why that gnome looks weirdly like one of our town's most famous sons?"

Damn it. So much for thinking that was just his own imagination running wild.

"Coincidence?" Murphy heard the obvious lie in his voice.

"If you don't want to do it, I'll ask someone else, but it seems to me..." Griff hesitated. "This might be good for you."

"Or the worst thing that ever happened to me," Murphy said. And okay, maybe that was a huge exaggeration, but then there was the way Jem had looked at him last night. He couldn't forget it. He was going to fixate on that single look forever.

What if Jem ever did more than look?

One of Griff's eyebrows rose. "That bad, huh?"

"You weren't around then, were you?"

Griff shook his head. "I thought so," Murphy said. "Jem's always been the golden boy. And I'm...well...*not*."

Reaching out, Griff patted him on the shoulder. "Maybe back then, yeah. But not anymore. Your gnomes are famous. You know that."

He did know that, and yet somehow, it didn't make much difference when they were discussing *Jeremiah Knight*.

"You shouldn't sell yourself so short," Griff added.

"You're just trying to get me to agree," Murphy said, chuckling.

"Well, *yeah*, but also...seriously. You're the most famous gnome carver on the eastern seaboard. That's why I asked you. I'm giving Jem the best this town's got."

"And because I'm available," Murphy said.

Griff grinned. "That, too."

"I'm doing a few meet and greets at the arts and crafts fair and doing a demonstration one day. I can't do any events that interfere with that. Tasha would kill me."

"Tasha would kill *me*," Griff said. "But no, that shouldn't be an issue. I'll email you a list of the events I need you at. Or..." He shot Murphy a teasing look. "The events *Jem* needs you at."

"Remember how you said you weren't a matchmaker?" Murphy reminded him.

Griff nodded.

"Keep remembering that."

"Do you remember Jem Knight?" Murphy asked Tasha later that afternoon when they were checking the inventory they were going to be transporting to the arts and crafts festival starting in a few weeks.

Tasha looked up at him in disbelief. "Do I remember *Jem Knight*? Jeremiah Knight? The defensive end for the Charleston Condors? The most popular kid in our high school class? Who's the most goddamn famous person who ever came out of this town?"

"Yes, okay. Stupid question."

"What about Jem?" Tasha asked. "You know he's back in town, right? He saved Griff's bacon with the festival."

"I heard," Murphy said dryly. And then because he was in for a penny, he might as well go in for a pound. "We ran into each other at Frosty's the other night."

"Oh?" Tasha glanced over at him. "And?"

"Nothing just...it was a thing. Or actually, not a thing. No big deal." Murphy wished he didn't sound so goddamn flustered like something had actually happened, when in fact, nothing had. Jem had flirted with him because he was in town and clearly bored, and Murphy had let him until the point when he'd become so charmed he'd done the only thing he could: run away.

He hadn't even had the balls to tell Jem who he really was.

Because if you did, all that flirting? Would dry up faster than the freaking Sahara.

"Kinda sounds like it was a big deal," Tasha said and flopped down on the ancient couch he'd set up in one corner of his shop.

Your studio, Tasha would remind him. *Words have power, and we want to remind people you're an artist.*

Was he really, though?

He was just Murphy Clark, who liked to carve stuff.

"I just hadn't really seen him since he left town." Murphy tried to prevaricate, but Tasha had been with him for all of it. At the beginning of high school, when he'd pulled away from Jem because he hadn't known what else to do, because *surely*, now that Jem was becoming popular, it was inevitable he'd do it, so it was better for Murphy to do it first. And then in the aftermath, when he'd been so sad and maybe even a little heartbroken over it.

She'd told him then that he was being an idiot.

He had a feeling that now she'd say the exact same thing.

"Don't be an idiot," Tasha said.

Okay then.

"I've done nothing idiotic," Murphy said with as much dignity as he could muster. *Other than flirting with Jem and refusing to tell him my name.*

Tasha did not look convinced. "You've been doing idiotic stuff when it comes to Jem since you were a teenager. I can't imagine that's going to change any time soon."

"Fair," Murphy had to admit. "That's fair."

"I told you back then you were being stupid, and now you're still being stupid about him." Tasha sounded very certain of this, and she didn't even know how stupid he had really been.

"He didn't know who I was," Murphy admitted. "He didn't recognize me."

Tasha glanced up from her tablet, looking him up and down.

Okay, he'd put on some weight and muscle since high school. And then there was the beard.

But he didn't look *that* different, did he?

Jem looked the same. A little bigger maybe, but just as handsome. Just as irresistible.

The only conclusion Murphy could come to was that he hadn't really changed that much, but Jem had just forgotten him. That seemed impossible to believe, but then he didn't know what else to think.

"Honey," Tasha said slowly, "you look *completely* different. If I hadn't spent the last fifteen years with you in my pocket, I wouldn't recognize you either."

"Really?"

Tasha rolled her eyes. "You put on fifty pounds of muscle. You grew at least a foot. Then there's your beard. Takes away your sweet baby face." She reached up and found his chin under all his beard and waggled it.

"Stop it," Murphy said, but he felt lighter than he had in days.

Maybe Jem *hadn't* forgotten him after all.

"So what else happened?" Tasha asked casually, but her eyes were gleaming with interest.

"Well, uh...he didn't recognize me, like I said, and so I just..." Murphy swallowed hard. "Let him flirt with me. A lot."

"He *what*?" Tasha sounded shocked. She set down the tablet on the table and before Murphy knew it, he had his arms full of his best friend.

She hugged him hard before letting him go. "I'm so happy for you, Murph," she said in a heartfelt tone. "You deserve this."

"I don't know what I deserve, but nothing's happening. Nothing *happened*."

"Why not?"

Ugh, the answer to that was too embarrassing, but then this was Tash, so she'd probably guess anyway. "Because I left," Murphy admitted.

"Of course you did. Why?" Tasha picked the tablet back up, scrolling through the inventory.

Why had he left? Because he was terrified, first off. And second off, because he'd wanted to tell Jem the truth about who he was, who they'd been to each other, and he hadn't known *how*.

Jem, who'd been his oldest friend.

Jem, who'd left him behind.

But you left him behind first, Tasha would say. It wasn't like she hadn't already yelled at him about it dozens of times.

"I was scared," Murphy admitted.

Tasha's smile was quiet and the look in her eyes sympathetic. "Of course you were. You never saw yourself properly. Even now. You shouldn't be afraid of Jem."

"Why not? He's the big shot he was always going to be," Murphy retorted. But then, that was unfair to Jem, too. Yeah, he'd made it to the NFL and become rich and famous beyond anything that probably anyone but Jem had imagined. But he wasn't smug or egotistical. He'd never rubbed his success into anyone's face.

Sure, Jem hadn't come back to Christmas Falls much, but then, he'd never made any pretense about wanting to stay either. And, when the festival committee had called him up, Griff had said he'd said yes to their invitation almost immediately.

"You're being unfair to yourself, and certainly being unfair to Jem," Tasha said firmly. "He's not a snob and you're not a nobody. And even if you were, you'd still be worth his time and his attention."

"Well, about that..." Murphy trailed off. "Griff came to see me yesterday. He wants me to like...hang out with Jem during events. *Officially*, even. Be a 'liaison' for the festival committee."

"Please tell me you told him yes," Tasha said.

"Well, I certainly couldn't tell him *no*. This is Griff we're talking about," Murphy said, trying to sound like he hadn't both desperately wanted to say yes and also, equally desperately, wanted to say no.

"Good," Tasha said.

"I'm just going to do what Griff asks me to do," Murphy said, trying not to sound defensive—or hopeful.

Because hope? Hope that Jem might cash in all those promises he'd been making with his bedroom eyes Saturday night? That was the real killer.

That was the thing that might actually break his heart completely.

Chapter 3

"So, how's the holiday cheer explosion?" Deacon asked, sounding not exactly cheerful, but more upbeat than Jem had heard him in awhile.

Beating the New Orleans Saints on the road probably helped.

Tell me the truth, Jem wanted to demand from his best friend. *Tell me what you don't want to say. That you're done playing. And I probably am. That the Piranhas game was the last snaps we'll ever take together.* But he didn't. They talked about everything else. Literally *everything* else. But not this. Not this hugely important, impossible-to-miss elephant in the corner of the room.

"Not surprisingly, an explosion of holiday cheer," Jem said dryly, juggling the phone as he unlocked the door to the cabin he was staying in during his time in Christmas Falls. His parents had wanted him to stay with them, but the festival committee rented this little house, one of the Snowman Cottages, for their honorary grand marshal to stay in every year throughout the season. Jem had decided even though he absolutely loved his parents, he did not want to spend the entire six weeks in their pocket.

So, he'd taken the house.

It was tiny and adorable and packed to the gills with Christmas decor.

The sheer amount of glitter would've given Deacon nightmares.

As for Jem, he just kept the lights turned down low, or else he'd probably get a migraine from all the goddamn shininess.

"And are they totally fucking disappointed they got you, who's a grump on your best day, instead of someone who actually *likes* the holidays?" Deacon asked archly.

Jem collapsed on the couch.

"The jury's still out on that," Jem said. "I haven't had to do anything yet. Not til next week, when the festival kicks off with the tree lighting."

"Don't tell me they're gonna let you light the damn tree," Deacon said.

"Thank God, *no*. That's all the Mayor's job. I'm sure I'll have to get up there on stage and pretend I'm happy to be there."

"Maybe..." Deacon hesitated, humming under his breath.

"What," Jem snapped.

His temper was shorter than normal. It was everything he and Deacon weren't saying since his injury and *then* there was the Murphy problem. Was it a problem? A non-problem? Jem didn't know. And that was a problem all by itself.

"Maybe you could actually *be* happy to be there," Deacon said bluntly.

Jem didn't know what to say.

"It seems to me that's the easiest solution," Deacon continued. "How bad could it be, eating gingerbread cookies and drinking hot cocoa and spiced wine and having everyone in town applaud you for a month?"

"That's not the problem," Jem grumbled.

"Then what's the problem?"

"I wouldn't have minded coming back here," Jem said impatiently, shooting to his feet and beginning to pace in the tiny living room, avoiding a life-size Santa in one corner and the coffee table in the middle, loaded with miniature elves, all looking like they'd been dipped in sparkles. "Except I'm coming back here thinking..." He cleared his throat. Realizing a second too late what he'd been about to say. *Except I'm coming back here thinking I'm not gonna play again. I'm coming back here thinking I may be coming back here forever. I thought I might be ready, but I'm not. Not when our redemption story got cut short.*

God, they really needed to fucking kill that goddamn elephant, but Jem didn't know how to say it.

Where to even begin.

"Thinking..." Deacon prompted.

But Jem stayed silent.

Deacon finally sighed. "You forget, I know you too freaking well. I know what you're thinking."

"Maybe you should say what *you're* thinking, then," Jem retorted.

"I guess it's time," Deacon said. "I'm going to retire after this year."

Jem let out his breath in a long, painful gust. He'd known, of course, but it was different hearing it. "I know," he said.

"What? You *knew*, why didn't you say—"

But Jem didn't let Deacon get the rest of the sentence out. "I know you, too, you know."

"Oh. *Oh.* Then that's why—"

"Yeah," Jem said shortly. "Yeah. I'm fucking mourning our last year together, okay? The season you asked for, that I gave you, and now...*fuck*. It's not gonna happen."

Deacon didn't say anything.

"I don't know if I even *want* to do this anymore," Jem said. "I was ready to call it quits after last year, but then you persuaded me, and I thought, well, shit, I don't have anything else to do with my life so might as well. And now it's weird, 'cause everything's different since then. I can't just...make my goddamn peace with it anymore. I'm resentful as hell."

"I'm sorry," Deacon said and sounded like he meant it.

"Yeah, well, not your fault. It's *nobody's* fault. Nobody for me to even be pissed at." Jem chuckled under his breath, more amused at the irony than actually finding anything about their situation funny.

"No joke," Deacon said. Then he paused again and in a much more serious voice asked, "So, you're not mad at *me*, then?"

"At you? How can I fucking be mad at you?"

"For asking you to come back and then you got injured—"

"No. *No.* It's not your fault. Freak injury. You know that."

"And not angry that I'm retiring, anyway?"

"Deac, you played the game your way, your whole career. If you know you're done, then you're done. I get it. I'm..." Jem trailed off because his throat got tight at the thought. The same way he saw Deacon was done, he saw it in himself.

It was just acknowledging it that was the problem.

The acknowledging and the figuring out what the fuck he was going to do next.

He was sure as hell not going to spend the next fifty years of his life in Christmas Falls, being applauded wherever he went.

He'd rather tear his triceps a hundred more times.

"I get it," Deacon said.

"Yeah, you would," Jem agreed.

For a minute, they just sat quietly. Not speaking. Just breathing.

Jem was trying not to let the emotions overwhelm him, and he had a feeling Deacon was struggling the same way.

"Just…I never expected it would turn out this way," Deacon finally said, breaking the silence.

"Me neither." Jem sighed. "What are you gonna do, you know, *after*?"

Because that was how he was already thinking of this: his life, divided abruptly into *Before* and *After*.

"Not sure yet," Deacon said, sounding thoughtful. Not angry or bitter or resentful about it. Not like Jem. *That's because he got to choose, and you never got to choose.* "But something to do with the Condors. That's all I know. Grant told me I'd be welcome here. Not as a job. Not sure I wanna be a coach or a scout. Just…to be here."

Jem didn't even bother giving his friend shit over *Grant*. For once.

Besides, he had his own theories, which he wasn't going to share with Deacon, over the whole retirement thing.

Because once Deacon was no longer playing for the Condors, Grant Green would no longer be his boss.

And who knew what would happen then?

Jem wouldn't count on Deacon's crush going unrequited forever—not that he'd ever mentioned it, explicitly, to Jem. He wouldn't. He was too private for that.

And Grant Green, the owner of the football team Deacon played for, was too off-limits.

"Of course you'd still be welcome at the Condors," Jem said. Which, as far as he was concerned, was taking it easy on his friend.

"I'm not even going to ask what that means," Deacon grumbled.

"Because you already know," Jem countered.

"What about you?" Deacon asked, clearly changing the subject. And Jem let him have it, because he loved the guy. Entirely platonically, but still. "What are you gonna do when you retire? Go up in the booth? Make a podcast? Start a business and plaster your dumb face all over?"

And that was the problem, wasn't it?

He didn't want to do *any* of those things.

His idea of hell was making nice with the media *once* a week—never mind every single day of the rest of his life.

"None of the above?"

"Well, I'm sure you're gonna figure it out, and whatever you do, it's gonna be completely fucking brilliant and completely fucking *you*," Deacon said, sounding very sure, *much* more sure than Jem himself.

"Thanks," Jem said dryly.

"And you know you can call me whenever?"

"I'm not sitting here alone, ready to have a mental breakdown in this town," Jem retorted. "If anything, I'm not gonna be alone, *ever*."

"Yeah?"

Jem made a frustrated noise. He hadn't intended to tell Deacon about Murphy, because really, what was there to tell?

"They assigned this guy to be my...I don't fucking know...*minder*? While I'm here."

"Like Carter's kind of minder?"

"No. *No*."

That was especially not true because the last Jem had seen of Carter and his "minder", he'd been fairly sure they'd be fucking soon.

He was not going to be fucking Murphy.

Or Murphy fucking him.

"By the way, speaking of Carter and his minder, they're—"

"Fucking?" Jem supplied. "That wasn't hard to predict *at all*."

"Actually, I think it's way more than that. I think they might actually love each other." Deacon sounded mystified.

"Huh. Well, good for Carter."

"Don't change the subject again," Deacon complained. "Who's this minder and why does he have you all tied up in knots?"

"How do you know..." Jem trailed off. He knew why Deacon had sensed it. Deacon *knew* him. "We went to school together. Were friends forever, then high school happened, and we just sort of drifted apart. But I ran into the guy at Frosty's and didn't recognize him, and he didn't tell me his name. I didn't realize it was him until after he left."

"And?" Deacon asked, like he already knew there was more to the story than Jem was telling.

"I don't know, why didn't he fucking tell me who he was? We were *best friends* for fifteen years. And now he's gonna be, I don't know, leading me around like a lost little duckling."

"You were best friends and you didn't recognize him?"

"Your judgment isn't necessary or helpful," Jem grumbled. "He's changed a lot, okay? Got bigger. Taller. Grew a beard."

"Right. Okay. So you...what? Hit on him? I didn't know lumberjack was your type."

"You'd be surprised." Jem had sure been surprised.

"So he's going to be your big daddy duckling. Not a big deal if you like him. And since you're you, it's probably mutual." Like it was all that easy. Like Deacon hadn't been angsting over his own crush for months now.

"But he didn't tell me who he was. He let me hit on him, and he didn't say a fucking word," Jem argued. "He might *hate* me now."

"Did you fuck him up in high school?"

"*No*, of course I didn't." Jem would've been outraged but he could hear Deacon laughing on the other end of the line. "I didn't fuck him up *or* fuck him. Or anything that would make him hate me now."

Deacon was smiling. Jem couldn't see it, but he could freaking sense it. "Guess you're gonna have to talk to him about it then."

"You're the worst," Jem said.

"Because I told you to communicate like an adult human being? Horrible! How dare I!"

But before Jem could argue, Deacon continued. "You know, I told you to actually *enjoy* this time. Be happy about it. No reason you can't use Mr. Lumberjack to make that possible. Rekindle...I'd say friendship, but we both know that's not all you're interested in."

"Asshole," Jem retorted, but fondly.

"But at least I'm *your* asshole," Deacon replied.

That was true.

"And that's not changing," Deacon added in a softer, more serious voice. "You know that, right?"

"That we're in this together, for life? Yeah. I do." He did. The one thing Jem had never ever worried about was losing his best friend.

You know...not like he had before. With Murphy.

Ugh.

"I'm gonna have to talk to him, aren't I?" Jem asked.

"Yep." Deacon sounded very smug about this.

Jem was not looking forward to it. Or Deacon's inflated ego when he probably turned out to be right.

"And," Deacon added, "text me and tell me how it goes, okay? I'm curious now about you and Mr. Lumberjack."

Jem sighed. "Fine."

After he hung up with Deacon, he fell back onto the couch.

He already calls him Mr. Lumberjack and he doesn't even know he carves wooden gnomes for a living. Wait til he hears about that.

And Jem realized that he would be telling his best friend more about Murphy. Not because he'd promised he would, but because he *wanted* to.

CHAPTER 4

JEM FELT LIKE AN idiot.

He was standing next to Mayor Grayson, waving like a total imbecile to the crowd gathered in front of the small stage, and behind them was the enormous real tree strung with dozens of strands of lights that would sparkle once the Mayor hit the button to light the tree and officially kick off the Christmas Falls festival.

He hadn't seen Murphy yet—though he knew he was supposed to be here.

He'd wanted to at least talk to him about that. Had Murphy requested the position? Or had Griffin volunteered him?

The only thing Jem knew for sure was he didn't want Murphy to hang out with him unless he wanted to—but then he wasn't up here on this goddamn stage out of desire, either.

Maybe you could actually be happy to be there. Deacon's admonition echoed in Jem's brain and a wave of guilt immediately swamped him.

He turned and waved to the group to the right of him, despite the feeling that he must look like a total dick up here, pretending like he was so great when the reality was so different.

The Mayor leaned over, and she was grinning. "I feel like they're more excited to see you than they are to see me," she said.

"Shit," Jem said and then internally panicked.

She must have seen his freakout because she laughed then. "Would it help if you thought of me not like a regular Mayor but a cool Mayor?"

Jem laughed with her. "Maybe."

He kept waving and discovered he didn't hate the renewed wave of applause and cheers from the crowd now that he wasn't just standing on the stage, semi-scowling.

"I definitely think they're here to see you," she said with a twinkle in her eye as she turned towards him.

"Ah, no, that's not possible." Jem shot her a smile. "I'm not the one turning on the lights."

"True. So how's it been, being back in town?"

How could he want to tell the truth and lie all at the same time?

"Uh," Jem hesitated.

"That good, huh?" She seemed good-natured about it, at least. "Well, I know Griff was very happy and relieved you could fill in for our grand marshal at the last minute."

"Yeah, a broken leg. That sounds rough." He knew the actor they'd initially tapped to be the grand marshal, famous for starring in dozens of Hallmark movies, had severely broken his leg on a shoot only a few weeks before the festival was going to start, and after hearing about Jem's injury, Griff had called, asking if he might be willing to fill in.

He'd said yes, not really thinking of what it would mean. Only thinking that he couldn't sit at home in Charleston, mourning the end of his season and his career, for one more minute.

To say he'd regretted it afterwards was an understatement.

But maybe Deacon was right, and this wasn't such a disaster.

He could reconnect with Murphy.

He could spend time with his parents during the holiday, for once.

Figure out what the heck he was going to do with the rest of his life.

He could do that here just as well as he could do it back in Charleston.

Better, even, cause there were some decent distractions here.

"It wasn't great timing for us," the Mayor said, "but your injury on the other hand…"

Jem laughed, which he didn't think he would ever do in conjunction with his torn triceps. "It worked out for you guys, for sure."

"You've been on Griff's wish list for a grand marshal for *years*, but you're always a little busy at the holidays," she teased.

"Guess I should've bargained harder," Jem mused.

"You didn't hear it from me," the Mayor said with a laugh. "And you should call me Mona."

But Jem shook his head emphatically. "You're not *that* much of a cool mayor, Mayor. I'm good with your title."

"Alright." She nudged him. "Do you think the crowd's ready for the light show?"

They all cheered.

"Light it up, Mayor," Jem suggested, stepping to the side so she could make her comments to the crowd.

He'd just spotted Murphy, hanging way back, behind the crowds, and he hoped that Griff wouldn't have a heart attack if he stepped off the stage.

He left right as the Mayor flicked the switch, and just as Jem had promised her, the crowd erupted when the lights came on, forgetting entirely about him, exactly like he'd hoped they would.

Murphy too, was distracted enough by the light show that Jem was practically on top of him before he realized he was there.

"Hey," Jem said.

"Hey," Murphy said warily, stuffing his hands into the pockets of his big thick plaid coat.

Mr. Lumberjack, indeed.

Deacon would *not* be disappointed, and frankly, Jem wasn't either.

It was a damn good look on the guy.

"You should have told me," Jem said.

Murphy winced. "Yeah. Probably."

"Not probably," Jem said and smacked him on the arm. *Yes, keep it friendly. Just two bros, reconnecting.* "Definitely. I felt like a total asshole when Mik told me who I'd just been talking to."

It didn't fix everything that Murphy looked undeniably guilty, but it did help.

Well, at least two of them felt bad, now.

"Ah, well, welcome back," Murphy said weakly.

Yeah, that wasn't happening.

Jem didn't think—just reached out and tugged the bigger man into a tight hug. Back then, Jem had been bigger and broader and taller, and now none of that was true, but Murphy still *felt* the same. Still smelled the same. Like pines and glue and crackling wood under endless black skies dotted with stars. Then something shifted. Was it him? Was it Murphy?

But it felt entirely different. Nothing like all the hugs they'd shared for fifteen years.

Was it the awareness of just how much bigger Murphy was now?

Jem hadn't thought, like the lumberjack thing, that was something that did it for him.

But before he could figure it out, Murphy pulled away, his head turned. Like he didn't want Jem to see how affected he was.

"It's...uh..." Jem stammered. *Do better*, Deacon said in the back of his mind. *You're so much better than this.* "It's good to be home."

Murphy glanced back at him. "I thought you hated it here."

Okay. Fair. He had definitely given that impression once or twice or a hundred times.

"I don't *hate* it, I just..." *Ugh*. Deacon was laughing at him now. "I was just busy. That's why I didn't come back much."

The corner of Murphy's mouth curled up. "You can convince everyone else, sure, but not me."

Right. Because how many times had he told Murphy, growing up, that he felt suffocated in this town?

"Would you believe me if I said being here is better than being in Charleston, feeling fucking useless?"

Murphy shoved his hands into his pockets. "Yeah," he finally said.

"Well, there you go," Jem said.

But Murphy still didn't look happy about it.

Or maybe it was that while Jem *was* in town, Murphy was now required to be his shadow.

"Griff told me about the uh...liaison thing," Jem added, when it seemed like Murphy wasn't going to bring it up himself.

"Yeah." Murphy's face had settled into hard lines under his well-groomed beard.

Jem winced. "You don't have to do it, not if you don't want to. I don't want to make you..." He trailed off and then cleared his throat. "I don't want to make you uncomfortable. Clearly, you're not happy about me being here. I don't want to make it worse."

Murphy didn't say anything.

Which was actually way worse than if he'd brushed off Jem's concerns.

Jem plowed ahead, even though Deacon in the back of his mind was screaming at him to just *hold off for a fucking moment.* "I'll talk to Griff, okay? I'm sure he's got some other volunteer he can—"

"No," Murphy interrupted him. "That's not what I meant. I said I'd do it, and I will. You're not...you're not terrible to spend time with. We were friends, right?"

"Right," Jem said weakly. "Friends."

He wanted to ask, *then why weren't we friends in high school? You brushed me off so many times.*

And then you stopped trying, Deacon retorted. *And you didn't waste more than a few moments feeling bad about that. You barely even thought about Murphy Clark until now, until Mik told you who he was.*

Okay, he felt a little—or a *lot*—guilty about how his friendship with Murphy had ended, now.

He'd been so busy, playing three sports and trying to parlay his football skills into a college scholarship and a way out of this town.

Too busy to take a spare minute to sit down and think about how Murphy had pulled away. Not until now.

"About high school..." Jem trailed off. Should he apologize? And for what?

He didn't even know what he should be sorry for. He just didn't like how guilty he felt.

"Water under the bridge," Murphy said gruffly. He reached out and patted Jem's arm.

"Alright." Jem wasn't convinced Murphy actually felt that way, but what else could he do? He couldn't force Murphy to talk about it with him.

Awkward silence fell between them, and Deacon was lecturing Jem on just how *shitty* he'd gotten at this, when the man next to him spoke up.

"The tree looks good," Murphy said, gazing over at the gigantic lit evergreen.

"I don't remember them ever being that big," Jem said, nodding.

"That's all Griff. He's an overachiever. Nothing's ever good enough for the festival."

"No pressure on me, then," Jem pointed out with a nervous chuckle.

"You mostly gotta do what you just did," Murphy said. "Smile and nod. Wave. That sorta thing. You can do that in your sleep."

"Not comfortably," Jem muttered. "If I wanted everyone's attention, I'd have become a quarterback."

"Except you can't throw a ball worth a damn," Murphy teased. Jem glanced over, smiling, the shared history rich and full and yet unspoken between them.

"Always threw it better than you caught it," Jem retorted fondly.

They'd tossed balls back and forth for years. And yeah, Jem hadn't been much better at throwing than Murphy had been at catching, but it hadn't mattered because they'd laughed and romped through huge piles of leaves and tackled each other into snowdrifts and burned their noses red under the bright midwestern sun.

For those years, they'd shared everything. Jem had known Murphy like the back of his hand. Now, though, he looked at the guy and saw a stranger.

But not entirely a stranger. Occasionally, there would be flashes there, of the guy Jem used to know.

It was those flashes that kept him rooted here, in place, trying to find some common ground again.

"I wasn't gonna be a professional football player. Not like you," Murphy said ruefully, like he was actually ashamed he hadn't been athletic when he'd been younger.

But Jem was looking at the guy now and there was no way he wasn't strong as hell.

He did *something*.

Was that something carving gnomes? Or single-handedly cutting down and hauling massive firs on the Milton Falls Christmas Tree farm?

Murphy looked like he could do both without breaking much of a sweat.

"When am I gonna see one of your gnomes?"

Murphy had the nerve to look surprised. "You wanna see one?"

"Well, *yeah*, according to Mik they're very popular and famous? You sell out every year?"

Murphy flushed. "Most of that is Tasha. She insists on keep-ing our stock for sale low so demand stays high."

"Tasha? Like Natasha Reynolds?"

They'd gone to school with Natasha and after Murphy had given him the cold shoulder in high school, Jem had seen him with her a lot. They'd become so close that for a long time, Jem had wondered if they were dating.

Had he been jealous about that? No, not exactly. More con-fused than anything else.

"Yeah," Murphy said, nodding. "She's my only employee, and well...I guess you could say she runs the business."

"Not you?"

Murphy laughed. "No. No. Definitely not me. I just carve the gnomes. That's all."

"Murph, that's the *whole* business," Jem reminded him.

"Except that's like claiming you were solely responsible for every single one of the Condors' wins and losses," Murphy explained. "Tasha and I, we're...we're a team. That's all."

"Ah, so you're uh...partners." And damnit, wasn't he still a little jealous? Over Natasha Reynolds, who he remembered was five foot nothing, had bright blue hair, and a nose ring. He'd never thought she was Murphy's type. AKA female. But maybe that had changed.

If Deacon could see him right now, he'd be laughing so hard he'd be busting a gut.

Not your finest moment, Knight, Deacon added.

"Not like that," Murphy explained patiently. "You know...you know I'm gay. I told you." He didn't have to continue, because they were both thinking it.

You were the first person I ever told. The first person I ever trusted with my secret.

"I remember," Jem said seriously.

He might've forgotten a few things, but he'd never forgotten that afternoon. The undeniable, unshakeable trust in Murphy's gaze as they'd huddled together in the Clark barn. The way his eyes had fluttered closed when Jem had pulled him close and hugged him for a very long time.

Less than a year later, everything had changed.

And goddamn it, Jem still wanted to know why.

"As for my gnomes, we sell some online. Some in the stores around town. Out at Milton Falls Christmas Tree farm. And uh..." Murphy flushed. "There's a big one, right out front in Sugar Plum Park they put up a few years back. It's not one of my favorites—"

But that was all Jem needed to hear.

He was already grabbing Murphy's arm and dragging him in the direction of the park entrance.

He couldn't remember if he'd seen a carved gnome when he'd arrived, but now that he was looking for it, Jem couldn't believe he'd missed it the first time around.

It stood in the central place of honor, right between the park and the temporary skating rink, set up to the left.

The statue itself was huge, at least seven feet tall, and as far as Jem was concerned, a freaking masterpiece.

The Santa gnome was smiling, but there was an amusing glint to his expressively carved face, his trademark hat looking like it was literally moving with his laugh as the pom-pom at the tip curved down and brushed his cheek.

The wood was dark and burnished, no doubt protected from the elements by many layers of waterproof varnish.

"It's not my best work," Murphy said, even as Jem stopped short, looking with awe at what his friend had created.

He'd always known Murphy was creative and unbelievably talented. But he'd never expected this.

"You've got *better*?" Jem asked in disbelief.

"You think it's good?" Murphy asked instead of answering his question.

Jem smacked him on the arm. "It's fucking brilliant," he insisted. "I feel like I could reach out and touch the fur trim on his coat and it'd be just as soft as I think it is."

"Ah, well...thanks," Murphy mumbled.

People were coming in and out of the park in a steady stream, and as he and Murphy stood there—Jem in awe, Murphy looking embarrassed by it—he couldn't count the number of people who pointed at the statue and took pictures of it.

And pictures *with* it. It was clearly a favorite destination to take a selfie.

"You're amazing, you know?" Jem said, turning to his oldest friend. "And you know what, I'm not even surprised, because while I might've left town, it was always you who were going places."

Murphy's face went undeniably red under his beard. The same color Santa's coat would've been, if he hadn't carved it so flawlessly out of wood.

"It was just...I was the right person at the right time for the job. They wanted a statue here, of some kind, after the big refresh of the park a few years back. Griff thought I'd do a good job."

"And you did a spectacular one?" Jem asked, raising an eyebrow.

"He thought so too," Murphy said.

"No freaking kidding." It felt natural to pull Murph into another big hug. "I'm so proud of you, man."

"Thanks." Murphy still looked like he wanted to sink through the ground, but he was smiling too.

"How long is your waiting list?"

"I sell a few I've made at the arts and crafts festival, and like I said around town. But custom work? Uh..." Murphy rubbed the back of his neck, behind the collar of his plaid coat. "Twenty months."

"Shit." Jem had wanted to ask him if he could carve *him* a gnome, maybe even one for Deacon, in matching Condors jerseys, but he wasn't going to presume on their barely repaired friendship. Less than a week ago, they hadn't spoken in fifteen years and while Jem might have millions in the bank and the fans' adulation in Charleston, Murphy was an honest-to-God artist in serious demand. That was another thing entirely.

"Why?" Murphy asked.

"Well, I just thought, I'd love to have one of those. Like in a Condors jersey, maybe. But you're booked—"

"No," Murphy interrupted. "I'm booked for the world. But not for you. Never for you." He shot Jem a small, uncertain smile. "You'd really want a gnome?"

"Are you freaking kidding me? That's the thing my garden in Charleston was missing. I just didn't know it."

"You'd—" Murphy paused and looked incredibly pleased. "You'd put it in your garden?"

"Hell yes," Jem said, meaning it. "It'd be an honor."

Murphy dug around in his jacket pocket and pulled out a little worn notebook and a pencil and began to sketch on a page, eyes intent on the paper, fingers suddenly looking deft in a way they hadn't only a few minutes ago.

This was the Murphy Jem remembered as easily as breathing. The kid who could get lost in his own ideas, in his own projects and art. The quiet sensitive kid who'd just loved the process of creation.

Jem hadn't quite seen that young kid in the big, brawny lumberjack he'd met the other night, but he could now.

"You want the guy in a jersey? Condors jersey?" Murphy asked without looking up.

"Yeah," Jem said with a nod. Maybe he wouldn't wear one after this year, but his years with the team—the best and most memorable of his career in the NFL—would be memorialized forever. It felt appropriate that Murphy would be the one doing the memorializing.

"I got you," Murphy muttered. He glanced up, and then just as suddenly as he'd started sketching, the notebook was tucked back into his pocket. "I'll let Tasha know."

"Can I see it?" Jem asked.

Murphy looked surprised. "The sketch?"

"Well yeah," Jem said.

"Do you not..." Murphy hesitated. "Do you not trust me to do a good job?" He was frowning.

"No, *no*, I trust you to do an even better job than I'm currently imagining. I just...I'm curious." *I want to see what you draw when you think of me.*

It was very stupid and absolutely none of his business, considering that their friendship had basically become extinct in the last fifteen years.

But Jem couldn't help but be a little curious.

Was it that flare of attraction to the man he'd experienced a few days back? Or was it the comforting warmth of the friend he remembered from his childhood?

He wasn't sure. Maybe it was actually both, mingled together, in a new and confusing configuration Jem didn't really understand.

Of course, just because he was still alone at the ancient age of thirty-three didn't mean Murphy was.

But he flirted with you the other night. And he liked it when you flirted with him.

That was true.

"I don't usually show the drawings to anyone," Murphy said slowly. "They're...they're not very good."

"You didn't think *this* was very good," Jem said, gesturing at the gnome statue in front of them.

Murphy's grin was unexpected and lit Jem up inside. It was the heat, yes, and it was also the warmth. It *was* both.

"You're just as charming as you could be, back before you left," Murphy said.

"I'd like to hope I've polished my skills at least a little," Jem said. Murphy hadn't brought up a boyfriend or a partner. There was no reason *not* to flirt with him. Especially not when he flushed so beautifully whenever Jem did.

"A little," Murphy teased.

"So can I?" Jem gestured towards Murphy. "Let me see, please. I promise I'll only say good stuff. All carrots, no sticks."

But Murphy shook his head. "Sorry," he said and sounded genuinely regretful. "You'll see your dude when he's done."

"My dude?"

Murphy flushed again. "Oh, that's just what I call them. Tasha teases me about it something fierce."

"I like it. It's adorable," Jem said honestly. He nudged Murphy with his shoulder. "Kinda like you."

"Oh. Oh. You..." Murphy trailed off.

"Yeah," Jem guessed, "I meant that the other night."

Murphy clearly couldn't see himself right, because he looked downright shocked. "Oh."

"Hey, you wanna go down to Frosty's? Grab a drink? Some dinner? Catch up?"

Jem thought maybe they could keep repairing their friendship. But Murphy reluctantly shook his head. "Sorry," he said. "I told a friend I'd meet him for dinner and some hot cocoa."

"Oh. Yeah. Sure. No problem. I'm good." Jem smiled, trying not to sound or look too disappointed. But he was.

He'd really thought he and Murphy had made some good progress, but there he was, running off again, like he couldn't wait to get away from Jem. Obviously Murphy didn't want to talk about what had happened to them in high school, but he was beginning to think that the only thing that would really fix them was to lay it all out. All the ugly shit Murphy wanted to ignore.

It wasn't like Jem *wanted* to air it all out, because he had a feeling he wouldn't be blameless, but anything had to be better than Murphy avoiding him.

"Well, I guess I'll see you around?" Murphy said. "What's the next event you, and I guess…um *I*…we're…at?"

"Yeah. Uh…I don't know what I'm doing next. The pie bake-off maybe?" Jem hadn't memorized the schedule. He'd sort of hoped he might see Murphy before their next shared event, but the way Murphy had said it made it clear that wasn't going to happen.

And again, Jem had to hold back the inevitable disappointment—and the curiosity. What had he done to Murphy to deserve this? He didn't know. He only knew that he was increasingly desperate to find out.

"That'll be fun," Murphy said, sounding like the opposite would be true.

Didn't that just *suck*?

"You don't have to—" Jem started to say. He'd rather intervene with Griff than force Murphy to continue doing these events with him when he clearly didn't want to.

But Murphy interrupted him first. "No," he said firmly, "I mean it. It'll be fun."

"Okay." Jem said awkwardly.

Murphy shoved his hands in his pockets again and turned to go. "Well, see you around."

Jem watched him go.

Not wanting him to.

And not understanding exactly why that was.

CHAPTER 5

"WHY DO YOU KEEP looking over there?" Arlo asked Murphy.

Arlo was one of Murphy's best friends here in Christmas Falls. He ran one of the more popular B&Bs in town—the Gingerbread Cottage—and even though they'd had dinner together last week after the tree lighting, he'd stopped by Murphy's house tonight and insisted he come out to the first social at the pop-up ice skating rink. *You can't just sit at home and mope,* Arlo had said.

Though, they both knew the truth, which was that Murphy wasn't moping. He was freaking out.

Over Jeremiah Knight.

"You know why," Murphy muttered.

Sure enough, even though he'd believed he was safe—because surely Jem wouldn't attend the ice skating social, not if he wasn't required to—there he was, in all his carelessly gorgeous, totally charming glory, laughing with Griff.

"You could go over there," Arlo suggested.

"Hell no," Murphy said.

"You can't avoid him. I thought you had to spend the next six weeks with him," Arlo pointed out so reasonably Murphy gnashed his teeth.

"Not avoiding him is not the same as seeking him out. He doesn't want to talk to me."

Arlo crossed his arms over his chest. "I thought you said the other night at dinner he wanted to hang with you and you ditched him. Which...I know I said it before, but I'll say it again. You can have dinner with me any time, Murph. He's *Jem Knight,* and I don't have to mention he's hot, 'cause you've got eyes."

"Yeah," Murphy muttered. "He's just...I don't know what spell he's under. But it's not gonna last, and then he'll be gone from Christmas Falls, and what am I gonna do then?"

"Know what it means to finally have the one who got away?" Arlo suggested, not unkindly. "Though if I believe Tasha, Jem isn't so much the one who got away as the one you *pushed* away.

Don't tell me you're doing that crap again. Him rejecting you isn't an inevitability."

"Might be," Murphy said. He leaned against the wall of the skating rink. He and Arlo had made several rotations around the oval, but then they'd stopped to grab two cups of Joel McArthur's fantastically spiced hot cider.

But the hot cider didn't change anything about Jem's presence, looming large on the other side of the rink.

"It's fear talking, plain and simple, and I get being afraid. I do. He's a big shot football player. But you're Murphy Clark. I'm sure you saw the picture."

It felt like the whole freaking town had seen the selfie Jem had taken with the Santa gnome and posted on his social media.

When had he taken it? Must've been right after Murphy had turned and left to meet Arlo, because the very next morning, there it had been. Jem had tagged his business, and everything, and Tasha had complained, good-naturedly, that if he kept up this flirtation with Jem, he was going to have to at least hire someone to answer the phone and email because they were inundated with inquiries.

"Everyone in the whole world saw the picture. You know that."

"Did seem that way. Hey, anytime Jem Knight wants to wander over to the Gingerbread Cottage and take some more selfies, I'd not complain."

"It's not going to last. He's not going to stay. It's just...he was always meant to leave, and even though he's here now, he's not going stick around. We all know it. He knows it. He's not even happy about being here. So him flirting with me is just..." The words burst out of Murphy, but then at the end, he couldn't even vocalize what Jem's flirting *was*.

Was it because he didn't know?

Or because he was afraid he understood very well and he'd never be able to turn Jem down if he was even a little bit serious?

"I didn't know you well in high school or earlier, so I can't say anything 'bout back then but Murph—you're no slouch. You're worth something. You want that guy?" Arlo gestured to where Jem stood, still laughing with Griff and Joel. "Then go get him."

"He doesn't mean it," Murphy claimed even though even he knew that argument was increasingly silly.

"I think the jury's still out on that one. But if that's true and he doesn't, there's nothing stopping you from convincing him otherwise," Arlo said gently.

"Ugh, I hate how logical you are."

Arlo gave him a little push. Murphy had spent years on skates. So many years, gliding around this rink. Smiling at the various people around town. When they'd been small, he and Jem had always come to the socials and terrorized everyone by skating way too fast around the turns and unbalancing old ladies—only to catch them at the last minute, because neither of them were bad kids. Just...preoccupied with their own need to go as fast as they possibly could.

"Go ask him to skate with you." At some point, Murphy had to think this was the only reason Arlo had dragged him out here. But if he said it, Arlo would just chuckle and shake his head. He'd never come clean. The matchmaking busybody. He should stick to his knitting circle.

But Murphy wasn't exactly sad about it either.

"Fine, only because if I don't, you'll never stop about it," Murphy grumbled. He finished his cider and pushed off.

His palms were sweating as he approached where Jem was standing with Griff and Joel.

Murphy tried to ignore how Jem's face lit up, so much like it used to, when they were just stupid kids, as he approached.

But it was hard, because it lit up something inside him, too.

A familiar feeling at this point, but not, as it had been for so many years, an unwelcome one.

"Hey, Murphy," Jem said.

"Murphy," Griff acknowledged with a tilt of his head.

"Good to see you, Murphy. I gotta go check on the cider," Joel said, walking away.

Griff melted away too, like Joel wasn't capable of checking the cider on his own.

If Murphy didn't know better, he'd say they were all in on it together, but Griff was way too busy with the festival to even dream about matchmaking.

"Didn't know you were coming tonight," Murphy said. He wished he'd come up with a better opening line on his way over, but then it probably didn't matter how much time he had on his hands—he was never going to be charming and easy like Jem was.

Jem raised an eyebrow. He wore a dark green knit cap covering up his dark hair, and he had a few days of equally dark scruff across his chin and cheeks, and with his smart navy peacoat and jeans, he looked like a fantasy out of every one of Murphy's daydreams.

Not the PG-rated ones, either.

"Because it wasn't on the event list?" Jem asked mildly.

And okay, it had been shitty how Murphy had tried to make it clear that they wouldn't be hanging out outside of Jem's official capacity.

Arlo was probably right; he'd been terrified out of his mind.

Scared that Jem didn't mean what he was saying.

Even more scared that Jem *did* mean what he was saying.

"Yeah," Murphy said. He should really apologize, because none of that mattered.

Jem had been a friend. His *best* friend. Even if nothing ever happened between them besides friendship, it would be good to get to know him again.

Though friendship's not really why you're over here.

At least he could admit that to himself, now.

"I'm sorry," Murphy said in a rush before Jem could reply. "I was kind of an ass, last time we met."

"No," Jem said. "Well—okay, a little. But I'm still trying to figure out why. Did I do something in high school, Murph?"

Jem had not been the first person in this town to call him *Murph*—and he wouldn't be the last. Arlo had just used his nickname a minute ago, and it had not affected him anything like Jem using it again for the first time in ages.

"No," Murphy said firmly. "You, you were yourself, Jem. Just yourself."

Jem frowned. "I don't understand."

"It doesn't matter," Murphy said, shaking his head. "I promise it doesn't. I'll—you wanna hang out?"

"Now? Tonight?"

"Yeah. I mean—I'm here. You're here." He glanced down. "You're not wearing skates."

"A-plus observation," Jem said dryly. "I haven't skated since...well, for a long-ass time. Probably the last time was with you, before I left town."

"Well, get some skates on," Murphy said.

"Can't we just stand here and drink Joel's cider and pretend we're skating?" Jem asked hopefully.

"Don't tell me you're afraid of making a fool of yourself," Murphy teased.

"Never, of course not. I can skate. I *can* skate," Jem insisted.

"Then let's see it," Murphy said.

This wasn't so hard if he thought of Jem as the kid he'd been. If he thought of Jem as he was now: big and tall and broad with a smile that promised sunshine and sin in the same breath?

Well. That was different.

So Murphy just wouldn't think of him that way.

He watched as Jem walked away, smiled and laughed with the kid running the skate rental, and then came back, settling on a bench on the opposite side of the rink wall to put the skates on.

His socks weren't quite the same, one gray and one bluish-gray, and Murphy's heart clenched a little. It was almost too sweet, too private, and he glanced away as Jem finished putting his skates on.

When he stood, there was a little wobble in his step, but this was also Jem Knight. He was a professional athlete.

If Murphy knew Jem at all, he knew he was probably reminding *himself* of that particular fact as he walked towards the entrance that led to the rink.

"You good?" Murphy asked as Jem stepped unsteadily onto the ice for the first time.

"Uh...yeah, I think so?" Jem wobbled again.

Out of total instinct, Murphy reached out and caught his arm. And then held on because he was pretty sure—like at least fifty percent chance—if he didn't, then Jem was going down and his ass was going to end up on the ice.

It was a fine ass and Murphy was just doing his civic duty to make sure it stayed intact. That was all.

"Well, I guess I was a little overconfident," Jem murmured as they took off at a very slow speed, Murphy still holding on to Jem, Jem still weaving unsteadily like Joel's cider had been full of booze.

"A little?" Murphy teased.

"I'm an athlete, you know," Jem insisted.

"Skating's like riding a bicycle."

"More like crashing a bicycle," Jem said, as Murphy navigated them around Mr. and Mrs. Golden, who were eighty-five if they were a day and were gliding along peacefully, like they didn't even realize how close they'd come to complete and utter disaster.

"Not gonna let you crash," Murphy promised.

"Thanks." Jem shot him a grateful look.

"Guess you haven't skated since high school."

"Think it was even before that. Last time was with you, Murph. Probably winter before high school. We were..." Jem chuckled to himself as he thought about it. "We were holy terrors, weren't we?"

"The worst," Murphy agreed. Those butterflies in his stomach were back at the utterly casual way Jem said *Murph*. Like nothing had changed—and everything, too.

"It's amazing they didn't ban us from the rink," Jem said, sounding so fond and affectionate.

He'd steadied out a bit as they rounded the last turn to make their first full rotation of the rink, but he didn't pull away and Murphy decided to follow his lead and just not let go.

Jem's arm felt so warm and solid under his fingertips. He'd feel that way everywhere, Murphy realized, and then nearly tripped on his own toe pick.

Whoops.

"You alright there?" Jem asked, the corner of his mouth turning up into a smirk.

"Perfectly alright," Murphy said. His own voice sounding slightly strangled.

"Is that your friend over there?" Jem asked as they rounded the next turn,

And sure enough, there was Arlo, beaming at him and *God help him,* giving Murphy a big thumbs-up right in front of Jem and God and *everyone.*

"Uh, yeah," Murphy said. "That's Arlo. I had dinner with him the other night, you know...uh, after the tree lighting."

Jem raised his eyebrows. "I thought you were single, Murph."

The most single. The singlest person to ever single. I promise.

"No, no, we're just friends. Arlo runs the B&B in town. The Gingerbread Cottage?"

"Oh yeah. He's a few years older than us, right?"

Murphy nodded. "We both like to uh...work with our hands."

Jem didn't bother to hold back his cackle. "Murph, you're gonna have to stop doing that, or else I'm gonna trip and fall and die. Or even worse, humiliate myself in front of the whole goddamn town."

"And they'll never let you forget it?" Murphy added with a nod. "Welcome to living in a small town."

"Hey, I'm the one who told you to get out, too," Jem retorted lightly, as they kept moving around the ice. But he'd known, even back then, when they were eleven, and he'd first felt the burning desire to get out and *see* something, to *do* something, that Murphy would never follow.

Christmas Falls was Murph, and Murph *was* Christmas Falls.

For the longest time, Jem had believed that wasn't him.

But now, he didn't know where he belonged. Was it back in Charleston? Was it here, now, in the town he couldn't wait to leave? Or somewhere else entirely?

Thirty-three was too young to be having a midlife crisis, but Jem didn't know what else to call it.

"Yeah, we both knew that wasn't going to happen." Murphy's smile was a little sad.

It hit Jem like a ton of bricks that maybe *that* was why their friendship had withered and died.

He didn't think; he just skidded to a stop, his skates sending up a puff of frozen shavings. Murphy, normally very steady on the ice but also not used to Jem's weight or it shifting so abruptly, teetered, wobbling back and forth, and for a second Jem laughed a little hysterically, because he could see it coming before it ever happened.

Murphy went down and took Jem with him.

Jem was still laughing, but now he wasn't the only one.

Murphy kept making these little snort-laughs that Jem remembered all too well. They'd been hilarious back when he and Murph were single digits, and they were *still* funny, but they were more than that now. They were absolutely fucking adorable.

Why hadn't he seen that back then?

Oh right. He'd been nine years old and cute was reserved only for the fainting goats that Murph's grandfather kept on their farm out in the country—not for big burly men in plaid jackets, laughing so hard they couldn't stop snorting.

"I wanna say," Murphy said when he finally managed to catch his breath, "that was *not* my fault. You stopped. Why did you have to stop?"

Jem looked him straight in the eye. People were weaving around them, giving them weird looks—which wasn't new at all, he'd been getting weird looks on this ice rink since he could remember—and the cold ice was beginning to seep through the ass of his jeans, but he didn't move. "Did you quit being my friend because you knew I'd leave and you'd stay?"

Murphy flushed and looked away. Began the process of slowly getting to his feet. Of course making it hard on himself, because he refused to use Jem for leverage.

Stupid, stubborn ass.

"You can tell me. We *should* talk about it," Jem insisted, climbing to his feet after him. He wobbled, nearly wiped out a second time, but out of sheer determination got to his feet and started skating after Murphy.

Murph, on the other hand, was actually still good on his skates, probably because he hadn't spent the last fifteen years on a football field instead, and he was already around the next turn.

"Goddamn it, Murph," Jem yelled. He had no problem pulling out all the stops and if that meant making a scene, he'd do it. Only if Murphy stopped running away and pretending that everything was fine.

Everything was *not* fine.

But to Jem's surprise, that tactic actually worked, because Murph turned and hit the edge of the rink, coming to a breathless stop.

"Why does it matter?" Murphy asked before Jem could say anything else.

"Why does it *matter*?" Jem was absolutely fucking incredulous he'd asked that.

"It was fifteen years ago, Jem," Murphy said, sounding reasonable. Except there was that wild look in his eyes that promised anything but cold, hard, solid logic. That told Jem there was a story there, even if he didn't want to talk about it. *Especially* because he didn't want to talk about it.

"It's not like it's bothered you for the last fifteen years," Murphy continued before Jem could keep arguing.

"You don't know that," Jem pointed out, but Murphy just shot him a look.

And okay, yes, there were years, literal years, at a time, when he hadn't thought much of Murphy Clark.

But then there were years when he hadn't thought much of Christmas Falls at all, except to be glad he was not stuck back in his hometown.

Even then, whenever he *had* thought of Christmas Falls, Murphy had never failed to cross his mind, a still slightly tender spot hiding in the back of his subconsciousness.

"I'm not going to lie to you or tell you something you don't want to hear. Like I missed you every day, Murph. There were lots of days I was so busy I barely had time to think at all. But before I even left, you were *gone*. Back then, yeah, that hurt like hell. I didn't like it. I didn't understand. I *still* don't. And that's why I'm asking. 'Cause I don't know to go forward, how to be your friend again, if you even want that too, without at least discussing it once."

"Is that what you want?" Murphy asked.

"To be friends?" Jem asked.

Murph nodded.

Okay, maybe that had been a lot of words. Words had never been his and Murphy's strong suit. They'd both understood that sometimes words were overrated. Probably why he and Murphy had always gotten along, from the very first.

But Jem was tired of not talking about this. Sweeping it under the rug wasn't working. It kept *bothering* him—and worse.

He kept feeling fucking guilty, and he didn't even know what he was supposed to feel guilty about.

"Yes," Jem said. Clearly anything else was asking too much. *And*, that voice that sounded so much like Deacon's added, *you're not even sticking around. So why does it matter if you want more than to be friends, now?*

But, Jem retorted, *I don't know that I'm not sticking around.*

Just like every time he argued with Deacon in real life, imaginary Deacon went annoyingly silent.

"Yeah," Murphy said shortly.

"Yeah?" Jem crossed his arms over his chest. He couldn't believe that was all the answer he got, after all this time. "Yeah *what* exactly? Yeah, you knew I was leaving and you weren't so you just said, what the hell, don't need to be friends with this asshole anymore?"

"Yeah," Murphy repeated.

"Ugh," Jem said. Threw up his hands in annoyance. "That was a dick move, okay? I thought I did something to you."

"I was a young, stupid kid, okay?" Murphy retorted, like that explained anything. "Were you any less young or any less stupid?"

"No, because I just let you do it," Jem muttered.

"Exactly," Murphy said.

That was the worst of it, as far as Jem was concerned. He could read between the lines—could still read between *Murph's* lines, even after all this time.

"That's all I get? *Yeah*?"

"What else do you want? Yeah, I felt stupid hanging around you, Jem. You were gonna be a big shot. You were gonna go places. Places I never even *wanted* to go, even if I could."

"You could've done anything you wanted to do," Jem argued, interrupting him.

Maybe they shouldn't be having this conversation with the whole town circling the rink in front of them, but at least this way, Jem decided, Murphy couldn't run away again.

"Yeah, and I did," Murphy said.

"Exactly. So let's...I don't know, let it go, okay? I left, and that probably pissed you off, some. You dropped me, and that definitely pissed me off." Jem paused. "Truce?" He held out his hand.

"Fuck that," Murphy said and pulled Jem into a big hug.

"Fuck what exactly?" Jem teased, his voice almost getting lost in all the plaid covering Murphy's shoulder. "The truce or—"

Murphy pulled back and shot him a baleful glance. "The truce, Jem. The *truce*."

"Okay, fine. *The truce*." Jem elbowed him and they pushed off the wall, starting to glide across the ice again.

"You good?" Murphy asked a moment later. "You're still a little wobbly."

Jem flashed his friend a grin. "You askin' if I need you to hold me up again?"

"No," Murphy said, making a face. "You're on your own. You didn't respect my assistance. You crashed both of us."

"Not the first time, and hopefully not the last," Jem said.

Murphy made another face, this one even more exaggerated. But Jem had a feeling he was smiling, deep down inside, where he couldn't see.

CHAPTER 6

Murphy watched as pie after pie was set on the long red-and-green-plaid-covered table.

They were in the heart of Sugar Plum Park, waiting for the annual Christmas Falls Pie Bakeoff to start.

"I don't envy you this," Murphy said under his breath, as it felt like ten more pies arrived next to the other twenty or so already spread out down the table.

Jem eyed the pies with trepidation. "I guess I shouldn't have eaten breakfast," he admitted, patting his flat stomach.

Murphy tried not to think of what lay underneath his maroon sweater. All those ridges of muscle with a trail of dark hair leading to...

"Yeah, you're pretty screwed," Murphy agreed, trying to snap his brain right back into the friend zone and failing completely.

Except, he'd *intended* to stay right there, comfortable in the friend zone, because despite how easily flirting came to him, Jem had made it clear he wanted to stay *just* friends.

It was only the day after the skating social. Murphy told himself he was already struggling because he was still trying to acclimatize himself to this new state of affairs.

You and Jem are friends again. Or at least you're tryin' to be.

The only fly in that ointment was the inevitable crush that had begun to overwhelm him in high school, that apparently had never gone away, only faded—and now, after spending a few hours in Jem's company, was back in spades.

But back then, it had been the heart-eyed imaginings of a boy who'd never done anything more than indulge in a few wet dreams. Now Murphy had been in relationships. Knew what it was like to kiss a man, to hold him, to love him. And the crush he'd always had on Jem was so much more unmanageable as a result.

Jem bent down closer to him. "Do you think they'd be angry if I went running and screaming in the other direction?"

"Running and screaming? It's *pie*, Jem."

Jem shot him a look. "But the *amount* of pie."

"Do you remember the time we stole one of Granny's fresh-baked apple pies straight from her kitchen counter? Grabbed two forks and just hid in the barn and ate the whole thing?"

Jem grinned, the smile lighting him up from ear to ear.

This, *this right here*, was why it was so hard to resist the siren call of his unmanageable crush. It wasn't just all their shared history, though that was part of it. It wasn't just how irresistible Jem had become as a man, though that was *definitely* also part of it. It was his fierce loyalty. His friendship. His humor. His intelligence, shining keenly out of his gray eyes. It was the big powerful body that maroon sweater was trying and failing to contain.

"Couldn't forget that," Jem said. "Or how we were sick for hours, after."

"Still worth it," Murphy said.

"Yeah, I'm afraid this is gonna be something like that," Jem observed ruefully.

"You just gotta take a bite of each one and then rank it on the scorecard here," Murphy said, gesturing to the one in his hand that Marlene, who was one of Griff's main festival volunteers, had handed him before going to round up the rest of the judges.

Mrs. Lil, who ran Yuletide Yarns, had been judging the pie bakeoff for so long she was practically an institution. She was legendary in Christmas Falls for her charity work and also for her taste in pie. The final judge was Joel, who ran Ginger's Breads, the best bakery in town. His being on the panel was the least surprising, since his aunt and uncle, who'd owned the bakery before him, had been exceptional in the kitchen and Joel was following right in their footsteps.

And then, of course, there was Jem. Not known for his charity work. Or his baking prowess. Or his taste in pie, that one apple pie notwithstanding.

Jem was eyeing the other judges as they approached.

"Do they *really* think I can judge pie as well as Mrs. Lil and Joel?" Jem asked him under his breath.

"No, you're absolutely here as the token rich and famous celebrity," Murphy said and then laughed when Jem made a face.

"Don't worry, honey," Murphy continued, as Jem continued to look totally panicked, "nobody thinks that you've got anything meaningful to say about pie."

"Thanks," Jem retorted.

"Young man," Mrs. Lil called out, "are you coming over here or not?"

Sure enough, Marlene had kicked off the contest by announcing the tasting was about to begin, to a handful of cheers from the gathered crowd, and Mrs. Lil and Joel were gathered at one end of the table, forks in hand.

"I'm going to start over here with the custard pies," Jem called out.

Mrs. Lil raised an eyebrow, and Murphy was pretty sure she'd mouthed the word, *amateur* to Joel, who'd just smiled.

"You," Jem said to Murphy, "are gonna do this with me."

"What?" Murphy croaked. "I'm not here to judge. I'm here to...liaise with you."

"Exactly. Griff said whatever I needed, you're gonna give me. And right now, I need you to give me some pie expertise. At least talk out each pie with me."

Murphy raised an eyebrow. "I don't think that's allowed."

"Murph," Jem said impatiently. "It's a pie bakeoff in Christmas Falls. This isn't an FBI interrogation. The score will be mine, I just—" He broke off. "I'm *not* qualified. Mrs. Lil is right. I'm an *amateur*."

"I think that's because you said you'd start with the custard pies," Murphy pointed out.

"I didn't even know *not* to start with the custard pies." Jem hesitated. "Why do you not start with the custard pies?"

"Cause they're heavy? Thick? Sweet?" Murphy shrugged. "I don't know, but there's a *process*. Mrs. Lil is practically a professional at this."

Jem sighed. Pulled out his fork. "Come on. I might not be a pro like Mrs. Lil," he said, gesturing with the utensil, "but that's why you're gonna be my assistant. Isn't that what all rich and famous people have? Assistants?"

"Fine," Murphy said, giving in. If he knew Jem at all—and he thought he still did, despite all the time they'd spent apart—there was no way he'd let this go. He was way too freaking stubborn. Murphy reached back to the table set to the side with cups, a water jug, and a whole tray of forks. He grabbed one and said, "Let's do this."

Jem grinned. Slung an arm around Murphy's shoulders as they approached the table.

On the far side, Mrs. Lil and Joel were already deep into pie deconstruction, murmuring comments to each other.

"First pie. This is a cranberry cream," Murphy said, reading the handwritten card in front of the pie, towering with perfectly browned meringue. Maybe if he focused on the pies, he'd be able to ignore the prickles of attraction sweeping up and down his spine at Jem's touch.

"Looks delicious," Jem said and dug right in with his free hand, still not letting go of Murphy—like if he did, he thought Murphy might escape.

What Jem didn't know was that as terrified as Murphy might be of his crush reaching monumental proportions, he loved this even more, and he didn't think he was capable of turning away now.

Whatever Jem wanted, Murphy was going to give him.

His attention.

His time.

His sanity.

And probably his heart.

"How is it?" Murphy asked, watching as Jem considered the bite of pie.

"Tastes even better than it looks," Jem pronounced. "Come on, Murph, give it a taste."

Murphy didn't need any more encouragement, and he dug in, grabbing meringue and the pale pink custard underneath with his fork, shoving it into his mouth.

He moaned a little as the flavors hit his tongue.

"That *is* delicious."

Jem shot him a hot look. "I think we just found our next pie to steal."

"Jeremiah," Murphy reminded him, "we have like a thousand more pies to taste. Hold that thought."

Jem laughed. "I missed you calling me Jeremiah in that tone."

"Your mother does it too," Murphy pointed out.

Jem's grip on Murphy's shoulders tightened a little. "I promise, it's not nearly the same."

"If that's your way of asking me to keep doing it, I wasn't planning on quittin' anytime soon."

"Good," Jem said. "Come on, we need a score."

"For the pie?" Murphy was a little Jem-drunk right now.

Understandably. Jem was in fine form this afternoon. So bright it was almost impossible to look away, even as the light of him blinded Murphy.

"There's all these categories," Murphy explained, waving the score sheet in Jem's face. "Texture. Creaminess. Firmness."

Jem dissolved into laughter, and Murphy wasn't far behind him.

"Are you two doing okay down there?" Joel called out.

"I told you," Mrs. Lil sniffed. "*Amateurs.*"

"We're good," Murphy answered.

But even as Jem plucked the scorecard from his fingers and began to fill it in, they both kept laughing.

"One down, a million pies to go," Jem said. "What's next?"

"Golden spice cream pie," Murphy answered, reading off the card, but still barely able to keep a straight face.

Especially when Jem chortled out loud. "Golden spice cream? Sounds...special." He waggled his eyebrows. Anyone else would look stupid ridiculous, and Jem did, but he also looked hot as hell. It was the easy comfort of their old friendship, with a bit of new spice thrown in.

How easy had it been to fall back into all their old patterns?

Way too easy.

Murphy discovered he couldn't even be angry about it. He was enjoying himself too much.

"I wonder what makes it that gold color?" Jem asked.

"Turmeric," Joel informed him. He and Mrs. Lil had made good progress down the table now. And he and Jem? Had only finished tasting one pie.

Whoops.

"You guys better get moving," Joel said quietly.

"Yeah, Griff's gonna have your heads if you don't get your tushes going," Mrs. Lil added.

"It's fine," Jem said. "Here, I've got the…uh…golden cream one done."

"Was it satisfying?" Murphy teased.

Jem shot him a look.

"Children," Mrs. Lil said with all the authority of a woman who'd spent her years organizing gossipy yarn store patrons, "are you going to take this seriously?"

"Yes, Mrs. Lil," Jem said, trying to school his face into a serious expression—and failing completely.

But they did make some progress down the line. After finishing the cream pies, they made it to the nut pies.

"Since it's been at least ten minutes since my last cream joke," Jem asked under his breath as he filled out the score-card for a pecan bourbon dark chocolate pie, "can I make a nut joke now?"

"I'd be disappointed if you didn't," Murphy said, chewing and swallowing a bite of honey peanut pie. He absolutely loved peanuts and this pie didn't disappoint. He nudged Jem. "Score that one high, okay?" he added, gesturing to the pie he'd just tried. "It might be the best thing I've ever put in my mouth."

Jem glanced over at him and raised an eyebrow. "Do I wanna know what kind of things you've been putting in your mouth, Murph?"

"Maybe you should ask what I'm gonna be putting in my mouth in the future," Murphy teased and then turned bright fucking red. Because of course he couldn't even exchange flirty comments with Jem without the fact it was *happening at all* turning him into absolutely embarrassing mush.

"Maybe I should," Jem said thoughtfully. But Jem gave him an approving nod as he noted down a very high score for the honey peanut pie—just because he'd asked him to—and that filled Murphy with a sweet kind of warmth totally different from the white-hot flame of only a few moments back.

"Are you two done yet?" Mrs. Lil asked archly. "Jeremiah, this is not that complicated."

"I'm a discerning man, Mrs. Lil. With pie and everything else."

Why Jem chose *that* moment to look right in Murphy's direction, Murphy didn't know but it was enough to make his face flame again.

Was it any wonder he'd grown the beard if even the barest amount of flirtation lit him up like a Christmas tree?

"So I hear, so I hear," Mrs. Lil observed.

"We just have the fruit pies left to judge, Mrs. Lil," Murphy added, trying to keep a straight, serious expression on.

"You two don't run off with the apple pie, okay?" she retorted.

Jem grinned. "You know about the apple pie?"

"Everyone in town knows about the infamous apple pie incident," Joel chimed in. "My aunt told me when it happened. A cautionary tale, I think."

"Your granny, Murphy Clark, was the best baker in five counties," Mrs. Lil said.

Joel nodded as Jem took a bite of cherry pie. "My aunt said she got her pastry crust recipe from Granny Clark."

"I miss her," Murphy said, because he did.

Even when she'd chase him with a wooden spoon cause he'd snuck a sweet treat off her kitchen counter.

But after the apple pie incident with Jem, he'd never dared to be that ambitious again. There was just something about Jem—he made you want to be bigger and so much more daring. Larger than life, just like him.

"I was sorry to hear she passed," Jem said.

Mrs. Lil whacked him in the side, and Jem let out a breathless laugh. "Could've come home when it happened, young man," she said.

Jem looked guilty. "I should've." He turned to Murphy. "I *was* so sorry to hear she'd passed," he said quietly, earnestly.

It was both the last thing Murphy wanted and yet also something he'd spent so many of these years craving—Jem's apology and his condolences.

"It's fine," Murphy said and realized he meant it.

"Still feel bad," Jem said, tucking an arm around Murphy's waist. Had they been this touchy-feely when they were kids? Maybe? But in the way kids were always carelessly touching each other. Not like this. Not like now, when every touch of Jem's lit Murphy up.

"She loved you. Was so proud of you. Always wore your college jersey on game days," Murphy said.

"Yeah?" Jem smiled. "I'm going to remember her that way, then. Wooden spoon in hand, jersey on." He paused, setting his fork down. "Oh my God, I think that's the last pie."

"You finished with your scorecard, *finally*?" Marlene asked, popping in.

Jem signed it with a flourish. "Yep," he said, handing it over to her.

"Took you long enough," Mrs. Lil said, but she was smiling. "So, Jeremiah, how was your first pie bakeoff?"

"I'm going to leave it to the pros next time," Jem said with a laugh. "You and Joel actually know how to bake a pie, so you should be the ones judging them."

"Don't tell him," Mrs. Lil said, even though Joel was right there and there was no question he could hear everything she was saying, "but that Joel, he makes the best pie in the county now."

Joel smiled. "That means something, Mrs. Lil. Thank you."

"Don't let it go to your head," Mrs. Lil warned.

But it was too late for Murphy to hear any of Mrs. Lil's warnings.

This whole afternoon had gone straight to Murphy's head and he was going to be walking around the rest of the day—the rest of the week, maybe even the rest of his freaking life—with his head swimming with too many intoxicating thoughts of Jem.

"So, I hear you judged the pie bakeoff yesterday," Jem's mother said as they sat at the kitchen table for dinner.

"Oh yeah, it was a good time," Jem said, barely managing not to blush in the process.

He and Murph had probably had too much fun together, doing it.

When Griff had told him Murphy would be accompanying him to all his official events, Jem hadn't imagined that they'd have so much fun. Or that they'd be spending quite so much time flirting.

Or that just the thought of Murphy sent all of Jem's blood straight to his cock.

Why had he told the guy he wanted to be friends again?

He should have told him the truth. *I wanna be friends and so much more.*

Jem knew the big thing these days were hookups and as Deacon told him laughingly, more than once, *friends with benefits.* But Jem didn't work like that. He couldn't get naked with a friend—and only a friend—and then go back after to just casual friendship.

He wasn't built that way.

He didn't know how Murphy was built, because he was too afraid to ask and hear, once and for all, that Murph just wasn't interested.

He sure seemed interested a few days back, when you couldn't stop touching each other or making more sexual innuendos than anyone would expect at a pie bakeoff.

Sophie Knight looked at him expectantly and Jem realized that she'd been talking to him. Shit.

"Your mother said it looked like it was a bit more than just a good time. That's what she heard from Mrs. Lil, anyway," Roger Knight said as he looked over at his son thoughtfully.

Without judgment, anyway.

Jem knew his dad didn't quite understand his bisexuality, but at least he'd never condemned it. His mom, either.

"And with Murphy Clark, too," she said, and there was no missing it. There *was* judgement now. In her tone and in her expression.

Over the fact Murph was a guy or...

"Jeremiah," she said firmly, "he's a good boy."

And there it was. They weren't upset that he was flirting with a guy in front of the whole town. They were upset that it was *Murphy* he was flirting with.

"And I'm not?" Jem asked, plopping mashed potatoes onto his plate.

"Jem, you've never made any secret of how you don't like this town," his father said bluntly.

"I don't see what that has to do with Murphy," Jem argued. He dug, maybe a little more forcefully than needed, into the slice of meatloaf his mother had laid on his plate.

"Just don't lead him on," Sophie asked softly.

"Is that what you think?" Jem was so shocked he could barely believe it. "You think I'd just—"

But his father, while accepting of Jem wholly and completely, clearly didn't want to hear exactly what he might do with Murphy, because he interrupted him. "We know you wouldn't *mean* to do anything. You two were always close."

"Until you weren't," Sophie inserted.

While he and Murphy had laid that ghost to rest, he still felt a stab of guilt at his mother's words.

"Bruce asked me about it at the garage today," Roger said.

"About me and Murphy?" Jem knew that the town gossip line moved fast but this was ridiculous. "The pie bakeoff was only two days ago."

"And you were all over each other at the skating social on Saturday night," Sophie pointed out. "Or so I heard, when I dropped some new wreaths off at Milton Falls farm."

"And Mik mentioned you two ran into each other at Frosty's," Roger added.

"Seriously?" Jem couldn't believe this—and he *could* believe it at the same goddamn time.

"You're big news in this town, Jem," his mom said. "People notice you. And Murphy's famous now, too, as well as being sort of tough to miss."

"It's not any of their business what I'm doing with Murphy—which is *nothing*, other than being his friend," Jem stressed, before his father could interrupt again and prevent him from giving the whole scoop.

Which yes, honestly, was a whole big lot of nothing.

Was that all he hoped might happen?

Absolutely not. But then, he hadn't anticipated that the entire town would be watching, either.

"I just wanted to remind you," Sophie said very gently, reaching out and putting a hand on Jem's arm, "that he's a good boy—"

"You said that already," Jem said, a little bitterly.

"*And*," she continued, "that he's got a good, gentle heart, and you don't need to lead him on if you're not serious."

"Who says I'm not serious?"

Jem didn't know *what* he was, honestly.

But then he didn't even know *who* he was anymore, either, so that wasn't a big surprise.

"That's why your father pointed out that you've never even liked this town," she said reproachfully. "Murphy's part of this town. An integral part. How can you be interested in him if he lives here and has no plans to leave?"

Jem didn't know.

But he did know that the last few days had been some of the best he'd experienced since the Piranhas game, when his triceps had torn and his season—and his career—had ended abruptly.

"We're just having fun," Jem said and knew how stupid that sounded. His parents were right. Murphy had a good, strong, *serious* heart, even if he could tease and flirt and dish out innuendos with the best of them.

What had Jem been thinking, even contemplating getting involved with him?

You were enjoying his company and having fun and not worrying for the first time in two months, Deacon reminded him.

But it wasn't enough.

Jem wasn't stupid. He didn't need Murphy to spell out what him leaving town the first time around had done to him. It was obvious, even if he never said it out loud.

Was he going to do the same thing to Murph again?

He didn't want to.

"Be his friend. He needs a good friend," Roger said.

"Does he though? He seems like he's got lots of friends." *And not many boyfriends.* "Tasha. And I saw him with Arlo Harper too. You two, apparently," Jem said, barely refraining from rolling his eyes. "Aren't you supposed to be on my side?"

"Always honey, and *of course*, we want you to be happy. To find someone who makes you happy."

"Just not Murphy Clark," Jem retorted.

"Not if it's going to break his heart," Sophie said firmly.

"You say that like it's a possibility. We're just…"

Sophie raised an eyebrow and shot him a look so recognizable it gave him serious déjà vu. He gave that look to *other* people. He didn't need to get that look! He hadn't done anything wrong, flirting with Murphy.

It was harmless. Right?

Okay. Maybe not *that* harmless, if the way he'd been feeling was evidence.

"Alright, fine," Jem ground out. "Message received."

Roger patted his shoulder. "We love you, son. You're a great man."

"Great," Sophie echoed.

"But if you're not sure Murphy's the man for you...don't toy with him, okay?"

Jem wanted to tell them both that he was a grown man. And Murphy was *definitely* a grown man—*so* grown, in fact. He didn't need protecting.

But suddenly he wasn't sure.

Murphy was also goddamn sweet. With that open heart, just like his mother had reminded him about.

Shit.

"Did you hear who won the pie bakeoff?" Sophie asked brightly. "Mrs. Lil said you were gone by the time they awarded the prizes."

"No." Jem shook his head. He'd dragged Murphy off to Jolly Java, claiming they both needed a coffee pick-me-up, when in reality, he'd just wanted to keep Murphy—and his blushes—all to himself.

"Martha's cranberry meringue won best cream pie, and Thomas' cherry the best fruit pie. And then Sasha's honey peanut won best nut pie," Sophie said. "She was over the moon ecstatic. I don't think she's ever won anything in the bakeoff before, and she's been entering for years."

"The honey peanut was good," Jem said. He almost said it was Murph's favorite, but maybe that was all the evidence he needed that his parents were right.

"I hear that," Sophie said. "Now, let's talk about Thanksgiving this week. I was going to make..."

As his mother started off on the recital of side dishes she was planning to prepare, Jem found himself going back to the afternoon two days ago.

How sweet Murphy had been.

As sweet as the honey peanut pie was, it wasn't even close to as sweet as Murphy. And as much as Jem had enjoyed the pies, he'd wanted more than anything to take a big bite of him.

But you won't. Not now.

Jem shoved the feeling of inevitable disappointment aside.

He'd lived with worse. After all, he hadn't really even considered Murphy for years. Surely now he could just move on.

CHAPTER 7

"YOU'RE SULKING AND IT'S going to scare away all the customers," Tasha hissed to him under her breath.

"I am not," Murphy said.

Except that yes, he was.

It had been five days since the pie bakeoff, and not a word from Jem.

It was a light week festival-wise because of Thanksgiving, and Jem hadn't had any required events so Murphy hadn't had any reason to see him.

Still, at the back of his mind, he'd hoped that Jem might *find* a way to see him.

But he hadn't.

Jem hadn't shown up at his workshop. He hadn't been to the holiday cocktail hour hosted at Frosty's either.

Murphy had stayed for the full time, and he swore he hadn't been imagining Mik's concerned glances when he'd sat alone and refused to talk to anyone for more than a few minutes at a time, even Tasha.

Or maybe it was because he'd had three sugar cookie martinis, instead of his regular beer.

He'd stumbled home and felt the after-effects of all that booze and sugar the next day, all through the Macy's parade and the dog show, and then the football games his father always insisted on putting on in the afternoon.

His mother had pointed out he was quiet, but Murphy had changed the subject instead of answering, knowing that it wouldn't matter in the end. She'd hear that he'd spent the night before at Frosty's, drinking too many sugar cookie martinis—but the only good thing was that she wouldn't know why.

Tasha, on the other hand, was smart enough to guess why.

"Is this about Jem?" Tasha asked, ticking off something on her tablet. Another gnome sold, no doubt.

"Of course not," Murphy blustered. "You know, I just hate standing around, like a great big boob who doesn't know what to do with his hands."

The arts and crafts festival was Murphy's pride and joy and every year, he encouraged more and more artisans in the surrounding community to join in and display their wares. Some just displayed, and others put what they had on sale.

Murphy, who was a little embarrassed at the prominent spot his booth was in—right as everyone walked into the event center, front and center so nobody could possibly miss it—did a mixture of both display and commerce.

He had some of his own favorite gnomes lining the sides of the booth. The gnomes he'd loved too much to ever sell. Then, in the middle were grouped all the gnomes Murphy had spent the year carving to sell exclusively at this festival.

It was only halfway through the first day—the only day Tasha required him to actually *be* here, because she said a lot of people came just to see him. He was always so awkward, which was why Tasha did the marketing and the selling, but he conceded this one point to her each year. He spent the first day at the booth and did two carving demonstrations throughout the ten-day run time because he'd realized his presence brought more people in and that was always a good thing for the rest of the artisans with booths.

"I know," Tasha said, patting him on the shoulder. "We all appreciate your sacrifice, showing up in public, once a year. So, your sulk isn't about the pie bakeoff and the absolutely ridiculous way you and Jem were all over each other?" She raised a magenta eyebrow.

"We weren't *all* over each other," Murphy argued. Maybe if he told himself that often enough, he'd start to believe it. At the time, though, it had sure felt like Jem couldn't get enough of him.

As for him? Well, he'd *never* been able to get enough of Jem Knight. Not as a kid, not as a teenager, and definitely not now.

"Not what I heard," Tasha said.

Jem had always complained about how this town never failed to stick their collective noses in your business, and Murphy hadn't ever necessarily disagreed with him—that was the joy and the curse of a small town, after all—but he'd never been at the receiving end of so much gossip.

He'd kept all his hookups strictly out of town for that reason, usually finding someone while he was away on business. It had only taken Jem Knight coming back to Christmas Falls to change his mind completely about in-town hookups.

In fact, he hadn't even considered the implications of it *once*. He'd seen Jem, and he'd wanted him, same as he always had.

"We tasted some pies together," Murphy said with as much dignity as he could muster. "That was all. You know I'm supposed to be going around with him to all these events."

"Yeah? What event are you two doing together next?"

"The parade," Murphy retorted before he could try to pretend that he hadn't completely memorized the schedule Griff had sent him.

"Ah-ha," Tasha said, shooting him a knowing look.

"Go sell some gnomes," Murphy grumbled. "I don't want to talk about my love life. It's a disaster, anyway."

Tasha's sharp gaze softened. "What happened? I don't need to kick Jem Knight's ass, do I?"

"Like you could," Murphy said with a snort. "No, he's just...you know...Jem Knight. For a second I thought maybe it might be different, but I was wrong."

"Were you, or is he a dick?"

"If you're trying to say he led me on, maybe he did, but I certainly didn't hold back either," Murphy said with as much dignity as he could muster.

"Should you? You wanted the guy practically your whole life." Tasha paused. "Don't you think you should tell him that, at some point?"

"No," Murphy said firmly. "Absolutely not."

He'd told Jem they'd stopped being friends because of Jem's inevitable departure—which was *partially* true. He'd omitted the part about having the most painfully hopeless crush in existence because Jem didn't need to know everything.

And he certainly had no business telling him that it not only had existed, back when they were teenagers, but that it had recently experienced an undeniable resurgence.

Especially not now, when Jem was apparently fine flirting like crazy with him, and then disappearing for five days at a time.

Clearly Jem no longer had his phone number, but this was also *Christmas Falls*, not exactly a huge town, and if he'd asked *anyone* for his number, they'd have given it to him. Or he could've stopped by Murphy's workshop.

Hey, you could've done those things too, a voice like Tasha's reminded him. *You could've shown up at his house. You knew he'd be spending Thanksgiving with his parents. They love you. You see them all the time. No reason not to stop by on a holiday.*

But Murphy hadn't, because he'd still been smarting from the three sugar cookie martinis and Jem not showing up to the cocktail hour.

"Murphy!"

He glanced up and flushed.

Because there was Sophie Knight, right there, standing in front of him like she *knew* what he'd just been thinking about.

Her son. In not entirely PG-rated terms.

She gave him a quick hug. "I thought you might be here today."

"First day of the festival," Murphy said awkwardly. "Tasha here always makes me show my face. Prove I'm a real person, or something."

"Or something," Sophie teased.

"I keep telling him that's *not* why," Tasha insisted, coming over and wrapping an arm around Murphy's shoulders. "But the guy doesn't realize what a catch he is."

"No, he doesn't." Sophie grinned.

"Did you come here for your wreaths?" Murphy asked Sophie, desperate for a subject change.

"Oh no," Sophie said. "I'm mostly retired these days. I just make some during the year for the farm, you know. If I had a booth, I'd have to actually take it seriously."

"Your wreaths are works of art though," Murphy pointed out.

Sophie just laughed. "They've always just been something to keep my hands busy."

"I thought that too, at first, with my gnomes," Murphy said. "But then I fell in love with them and—"

"So did the rest of the world," Sophie finished for him with a big smile, patting him on the arm. "I know. You're so talented, Murphy, and we're all so proud of you."

"Ah, thanks," Murphy said.

"I don't suppose Jem is with you?" Tasha asked into the silence that fell among the three of them.

Murphy elbowed her in the side, as subtly as he could. He did not need Tasha to start interfering.

This thing between him and Jem was already complicated enough.

"Jem? Oh, no. You know he'd rather cut off his own arm than come to one of these things," Sophie said with a light laugh.

Murphy winced. Hoped that Jem's mother missed it.

"I don't know," Tasha said. "I think he'd find a few things here he likes. Or *one* thing."

Murphy was seriously going to kill her.

"Oh?" Sophie sounded genuinely interested.

Or maybe Murphy was going to be the one who died, literally spontaneously combusting right here on the spot.

"It's like the saying goes, you never see what's right in front of you," Tasha said sweetly. "Right, Murph?"

"No doubt," Murphy said through clenched teeth.

"You ever come down from your sugar high, Murphy?" Sophie asked. "Jem wouldn't even touch pie at Thanksgiving, said he'd already had his fill this year."

Clearly Jem's mom had been trying to change the subject, and continue to make small talk, but *ugh*, did she have to bring up the pie bakeoff? She'd obviously heard about it.

Tasha said the whole *town* had heard about it, and if she was to be believed, everyone had been buzzing about it.

Murphy wasn't an exception. He'd ridden high for days after the bakeoff—and not from all that sugar.

"I'm good," Murphy said.

"But he could be better," Tasha added.

Sophie shot her a puzzled look, but instead of asking about it, said, "I've got to move on, but it was so good to see you, Murphy. Don't be a stranger. Jem said how much he's enjoyed hanging out with you the last few weeks."

"He won't!" Tasha called out as Murphy stood there, stock-still, not sure what to say as Jem's mother walked away.

He turned to his best friend. "Why are you like this?" he asked under his breath.

But Tasha had a completely innocent expression plastered across her traitorous face. "What? She said it, not me. Don't be a stranger, Murph. That means, get your fine lumberjack ass over to the Knights' one evening, or I know, Jem's staying in one of the Snowman Cottages, the one the festival rents every year. Do *something*."

Murphy considered, for a half a second, whining about why it had to be him. Why couldn't it be Jem? But he knew all Tasha would say was that he was a grown fucking adult, and if he wanted something, he should go get it.

That was undoubtedly true.

But even if he got Jem Knight, he wasn't sure what he'd do with him.

Lie. You know exactly what you'd do with Jem Knight.

"Tomorrow," Murphy said in a strangled voice, "I'll see him tomorrow. At the parade. And I'll...uh..."

"Not do *nothing*," Tasha said, elbowing him again. "Do *something*."

"Didn't I do something at the pie bakeoff? At the ice skating social?"

"You flirted around the idea."

"I don't know, I think I kinda flirted *with* the idea," Murphy retorted. "If the town rumor mill is to be believed, I practically threw Jem down on the ground and planted a flag in him."

"If only you had, Murph. If only you had."

"What is that supposed to mean?"

"I *mean*," Tasha said, "that Jem didn't get it. Because if he did, I don't think he'd just ghost you, like he has. Tell him you like him. Better yet, tell him you've liked him for twenty freaking years. That'd be even better."

"I'm not doing that. He doesn't need to know anything about my old crush. It would only make everything awkward," Murphy said bluntly.

"Honey," Tasha said, patting him on the cheek, "it's long past awkward."

Murphy made a face, but he couldn't deny she was probably right.

They'd undoubtedly made fools of themselves at the pie bakeoff, and yet Murphy still couldn't find it in himself to regret it—even if it meant the whole town was talking about it.

Even if he could barely look Sophie Knight in the eye anymore.

"Tell me you're at least going to do *something* at the parade," Tasha continued.

"I don't know what I'm going to do yet," Murphy said.

"You don't have all the time in the world to figure this out, Murph," Tasha said, which was a reminder Murphy didn't need. He knew Jem wasn't going to be here long and he also had a feeling he wouldn't be sticking around. This festival season wasn't Jem coming back to Christmas Falls and deciding he loved it here, after all. Nope, he was going to have to be okay having what he wanted with the guy and then waving goodbye at the end of it.

He'd made his peace with that.

But maybe...maybe Jem hadn't?

Murphy knew the only way he'd know for sure was if he asked him.

"I'll talk to him at the parade," Murphy said. Not sure if he was promising Tasha—or himself.

CHAPTER 8

IT HAD BEEN A totally shitty week.

All of Jem's plans about seeking out Murphy at his studio or "running into him" the Wednesday before Thanksgiving at the cocktail hour at Frosty's had been totally derailed by his parents sticking their noses right into his business and making him feel *bad*.

The worst part of it was he still wanted Murphy. No matter how bad he felt, no matter how freaking guilty and how much he *knew* he should keep his hands off the guy, he still wanted to touch him in the first place.

"Make sure to smile!" Marlene coached him as Jem took his place in a bright red Mustang from the '60s, strung with lights from the tip of its front bumper all the way to the back.

Jem gave her an admittedly weak one and she shook her head. "I know you can do better than that. Do I need to get Murphy up here on the float to get you to give me a *real* smile?"

Jem widened his smile on cue. No, he did not want to share this back seat with Murphy. That would be awkward times ten. It had already been difficult enough when Murphy had greeted him a few minutes ago with a huge bear hug that had gone on and on and on and yet Jem had wanted to go even longer still.

"That's better," Marlene said, giving him an approving nod.

He'd worried Murph might hold it against him that he'd ghosted him for the last six days, after the wonderful afternoon they'd spent at the pie bakeoff.

But Murphy didn't appear bothered—or deterred—in the least. He'd seemed genuinely thrilled to see him, even teasing him a few times about how Jem was now more important than Santa.

No, he was definitely not more important than Santa, he was just geographically positioned in front of him in the parade lineup, that was all. And Jem had every intention of telling Murphy exactly that, but before he'd gotten a chance to, Marlene had grabbed his arm and insisted they get him situated.

Just as Marlene was hauling him off, Murphy had called out that for all his hard work being more important than Santa, he deserved a drink at Frosty's after this.

Jem hadn't had a chance to say no—and goddamn it, he hadn't *wanted* to say no.

Then say yes. Go with him, and enjoy your stupid-ass self, Deacon chastised him.

If his mother lectured him again about breaking the heart of the town's favorite son, then he'd remind her that grabbing a drink with Murph could be *friendly.*

Also, Murphy might have that big, open heart, but he wasn't stupid either. He was an adult, he was almost definitely not a virgin—a thought that made Jem sweat, just considering it—and he knew exactly what they were dancing around.

Jem had had these six days to consider it, and Murphy had too.

He tried to settle into the back seat of the convertible, but he felt itchy. Eagerness, Jem realized. He was ready for this part of the evening to be over so he could cuddle up with him in a booth at Frosty's and maybe, if he played his cards right, discover if Murphy's lips were as soft as they looked, peeking out from his well-trimmed dark beard.

"You good to go?" Griff asked, stopping in front of Jem's car, leaning on the door. "Need anything before we get started?"

"I'm good," Jem said. "How do you do this every year? *Honestly.*"

Griff grinned. "It helps being behind the scenes. Mostly. Anyway, that's what I tell myself. Come on, it's gonna be great. You're definitely a favorite with the whole town."

Jem wasn't sure about that. In fact, he was pretty sure that was actually Murphy. Maybe they should've gotten him to be the grand marshal—he'd have actually enjoyed riding in front of Santa.

"You should get Murphy to do this some year," Jem said before Griff could turn and move onto the next entry in the parade.

Griff raised an eyebrow. "Do you think we haven't tried? Tasha has to work some serious magic to even get him to show up a few times at the arts and crafts festival, and that's his baby."

"The arts and crafts festival?"

Griff nodded. "He's doing his big carving demonstration tomorrow. Should be a good time." Jem swore the guy's eyes twinkled, surprisingly.

Was the guy matchmaking again?

Maybe.

"Yeah? Maybe I'll stop by."

Griff shot him a look before he moved on. Okay, Jem was *definitely* going to be stopping by and they both knew it.

Jem had only about thirty seconds before his driver started up the car to wonder why Murphy hadn't told him about the demonstration.

Surely he had to know Jem hadn't spent much time monitoring the festival schedule, other than the events he'd been asked to attend. *And all the other events you marked because you thought Murph might be at them*, Deacon added dryly.

The car began to creep forward slowly, turning onto the first street of the route. The sidewalks were lined with people, cheering and shouting and clapping. It was actually easier than Jem realized to wave back when they waved at him, their faces lit up with the electric candles they were holding and the light ropes they were wearing around their necks and wrists.

In fact, he was so busy waving and greeting the crowds, cheering excitedly for him, that it took him almost halfway through the parade before he realized why Murphy hadn't told him about the demonstration.

Because you've been avoiding him like an idiot.

Yep, that was almost definitely why.

This was a different flavor of guilt than possibly using and discarding Christmas Falls' favorite son. Because he'd done exactly the thing he hadn't wanted to do—drop Murphy again—and all because he'd been afraid.

Afraid of being the worst version of himself. A careless and thoughtless guy. But he wasn't that guy, especially not if he specifically chose not to be.

Okay, so he hadn't always been the biggest fan of Christmas Falls. Did he love it now? No, he did not. But now it had more to do with *himself*—the enormous jagged hole inside that he'd arrived with—than the town itself.

In fact, Jem could even admit, as they made the last turn down the final street of the parade route, that there were some things he even could *like* about the town. It was like a jewel box, shining brightly in the night with all the twinkling colored lights. And even he could admit that the way the town came together and generated income for the whole year with this one five-week festival, promising fun for the whole family and then *delivering* it, was pretty damn cool.

It was so rare to see an entire town work together towards one common goal, but in Christmas Falls they had one.

It hit Jem like a stiff arm to the face.

Christmas Falls was like a much bigger version of every football team he'd ever played on.

He'd wondered what he could do to replace the gaping hole of loss after retiring, but what if it was right here the whole time?

When the parade came to a close, Jem was still a bit dazed from his realization. Not just the fact of it, but that he'd never considered that possibility before.

You were young and stupid when you left this town. You didn't see it then, but at least you see it now.

"Hey, lookin' sharp out there," Murphy said as Jem climbed out of the car and Murphy greeted him.

It was probably part of his liaison work to be there to make sure he was okay after the parade. Griff had probably told him to be around in case Jem needed to ice his arms after spending the last hour waving constantly, but he felt fine.

Okay, he felt *more* than fine.

"You think I looked okay?" Jem asked, feeling suddenly self-conscious. What if he hadn't? Had the Condors scarf, bright with its red and orange, wound around his neck, been too much? He'd almost not worn it, because even reaching for it had pained him, but that was why he was here, wasn't it? Because he was Jeremiah Knight, defensive end for the Charleston Condors.

Murph shot him a look. "Hell yeah, you looked amazing." He reached over and fingered the scarf Jem had wrapped around his neck. "I like this, especially. Most people worship you, you know, but it's a good reminder to everyone else that doesn't that they *should*," Murphy teased.

"Yeah?" Jem smiled.

"Yeah," Murphy said with certainty. "Come on, let's get you a drink. You deserve it, like I said."

"I was only *geographically* more important than Santa," Jem said.

"Oh, is that the argument you're going with?" Murphy joked.

Jem nodded as they headed down the street towards Frosty's.

Not surprisingly, when Murphy pulled the door open, it was absolutely packed inside with festival goers fresh from the parade, and all of them thirsty.

"Shit," Jem said as they barely fit into the front door, the place was so full.

Murphy glanced over at him. Waiting, Jem realized, to see what he'd do.

Would he use his celebrity and his status to get them a table, possibly even kicking someone out?

Yeah, Jem might've not spent the last fifteen years in this town, but he'd never been a snob. He'd never believed, just because he was a damn good football player, that he was better than someone who wasn't.

"Maybe we should skip the drink," Jem suggested. But he was already disappointed. *Doesn't mean you can't ask Murphy to keep hanging out with you*, Deacon reminded him.

"Or we could get a couple of to-go cups and take this outside," he continued.

Murphy's face lit up. "Yeah, that sounds nice. I'll..." He gestured towards the bar. "Get through there. You want some of Mik's hard cider or maybe some boozy hot chocolate?"

What Jem had wanted was to cozy up in a booth with Murphy and a few beers and use the excuse of the booze to get touchy-feely.

"Cider," Jem said.

"You sure you're gonna be warm enough?" Murphy asked, glancing down at Jem's leather jacket, which *yes*, looked very sharp.

Jem grinned and then unzipped it. Showing the thick woolen lining and the sweater he'd put on underneath. "I'll be fine," he said. "And if I get cold, I think I know someone who might be willing to get me warm again."

"Yeah, I think so," he murmured, flushing.

How had he grown up around all of Murphy's blushes and never realized how fucking adorable they could be?

Jem patted him on the shoulder. "Grab us the drinks and I'll see what else I can dig up."

When Murphy met him outside holding two paper cups, Jem was carrying a bag of his own.

"What's in there?" Murphy asked curiously, as they set out, in unspoken agreement, towards Sugar Plum Park.

Jem opened the bag and showed Murphy. "I convinced one of the kitchen staff to give us some of their meat pies. Thought we could munch on them while we walked around."

There were still pockets of visitors strolling around the streets, but when they got to the park, the crowds had begun to thin a bit, especially because Murphy reached out and with a touch, nudged Jem towards the other side of the park, the one not currently occupied by the temporary skating rink.

Jem was relieved. He hadn't wanted to join the masses down at the skating rink. He just wanted some one-on-one time with Murphy.

"These are so good," Murphy said, biting into a meat pie and chewing with relish. "They put some kind of spice in that just makes it taste so different."

"I think it's curry, actually," Jem said, as he finished his own in a few big bites. Murph was right; they *were* delicious.

"Huh, I don't know if I've ever had curry."

It was a stark reminder of how different they were. There was an Indian restaurant in Charleston that Jem grabbed takeout from at least once a week.

But instead of focusing on the ways they were different, as his first instinct—and, he'd guess, his *mother's* instinct—Jem said, "I think you'd love it. You'll have to come visit me in Charleston some time, and I'll take you to my favorite place."

"Yeah?" Murphy grinned, looking absolutely delighted at the possibility.

"Yeah," Jem agreed.

Murphy steered them now to a bench, with wooden slats and decorative ironwork along the back and sides. Jem sat next to Murphy, shivering a little as his ass hit the cold seat.

It felt natural to just slide a little closer, right into Murphy's undeniable warmth. Murphy's arm went over the back of the bench, and Jem had done this move enough times to know what was coming.

It was only a matter of time before Murphy's arm would be around his shoulders.

Jem couldn't freaking wait.

"About that," Murphy said hesitantly.

"About what?"

"You kinda disappeared this week," Murphy said. "Why? Were you okay?"

Jem was surprised. The last thing he'd expected was for him to say anything—or to ask him why he'd done it.

He could lie. He could say he'd experienced a setback. He could say he'd had to go into Charleston for a checkup with his orthopedic surgeon.

But he couldn't do that to Murph. He couldn't make up a story just because the truth was uncomfortable.

"My mom told me how much everyone was talkin' about us, after the pie bakeoff," Jem admitted.

Murphy frowned. "You stayed away because you didn't like the gossip?"

"Not exactly," Jem said with a wince. "Worse than that. I stayed away because my parents lectured me about what we were doing together."

"Are you freaking kidding me? Your *parents* warned you off me? And you listened to them?" Murphy sounded more than a little outraged and Jem couldn't blame him.

"I know, it's shitty," Jem said. "And I realize now it was a stupid thing to do."

"For them to say anything or for you to listen?"

Jem winced again. "Both?"

"Yeah. Jesus. I can't believe Sophie would do that. Or Roger. I'm not a bad guy." Murphy seemed genuinely upset by the possibility that his parents didn't like him.

"Oh, it's worse than that. They think you're great. That you hang the freaking moon," Jem said. "It's me they're not sure of."

Murphy's jaw dropped. "Seriously?"

Jem nodded. He wasn't proud, but the only way forward that he could see, after their childhood friendship and then what had happened to them in high school, was for them to be totally honest with each other. Even if it was uncomfortable.

"But nothing even happened. Yeah, we flirted a little..." Murphy grinned. "Okay, a *lot*, but that's what I wanted to talk to you about—"

But Jem knew this was his shot, and he wanted nothing more than to take it.

"Murph," Jem interrupted him. "Maybe nothing happened. But it doesn't mean I didn't want *this* to happen."

And on a frigid bench in Sugar Plum Park, with the lights twinkling overhead, and snowflakes beginning to fall, Jeremiah Knight leaned in and finally kissed Murphy Clark.

Murphy had known it was coming.

Hadn't he planned it out so that it might?

The romantic light-filled park at night, the snow beginning to fall. His arm, wrapped around Jem's shoulders.

But he still couldn't quite believe it when Jem leaned in and kissed him.

Softly, carefully, at first, like he was afraid to spook him.

Murphy understood. They were outside, where anyone could come across them and yes, the rumor mill in town had already been going at twice its regular speed. He could've just kept it a nice, sweet light kiss, but he'd been dying to kiss Jeremiah Knight for more than half his life.

Instead of playing it safe, Murphy deepened the kiss, loving the way Jem groaned in his throat as they fell into each other. Feeling his heartbeat accelerate as Jem tilted his head and leaned into him like he couldn't get close enough.

Murphy hadn't had a ton of first kisses in his life, but as Jem's tongue stroked his own, he realized not only was this the one it felt like he'd been waiting his whole life for, but it was the best one he'd ever had.

It felt so normal and so right to be kissing Jem, like hugging an old friend—and yet, even more than that, it was also a heart-racing, exhilarating ride he never wanted to get off.

Jem's fingers curled into his jacket, the cold brush of them against his warm neck cooling him down, but also exciting him.

What would his strong touch feel like someplace else?

Murphy groaned as Jem's mouth slanted over his own, and he knew he needed to pull back, to get some perspective.

But after a whole life of perspective, it didn't sound like much fun.

Not nearly as much fun as what he was doing in this moment.

Jem was the one who found sanity for both of them and finally broke the kiss.

"Wow," he said softly, eyes shining like it had been as good an experience for him as it had been for Murphy.

And wasn't that additionally mind-blowing?

Maybe Jem hadn't always felt this way about him, but it was clear as day that he did now.

"I didn't expect—" Murphy cleared his throat. "Well, I hoped, but then you disappeared..."

"I'm sorry about that, again. I...I want to do right by you," Jem said seriously. "I know me leaving last time hurt you."

Were they about to have a breakup talk before they ever got together? God, Murphy hoped not.

"Yeah," Murphy admitted. It had hurt him. More than Jem had ever known—and that had been one hundred percent on purpose. Because if he had known how upset Murphy was, he might realize exactly why that was. And back then, Murphy hadn't been ready to admit his feelings.

"I don't know what I'm doing," Jem continued wryly, "but I do know one thing, loud and clear, no question about it in my mind."

"What's that?"

God, please don't say you're leaving. Not yet.

"I really like being here, with you." Jem's voice rang with confidence, and he reached over, curling his fingers into Murphy's and squeezing. "I like *you*. No matter what my future holds, you're in it somewhere."

Yep, Murphy had been waiting for that for a *long* time. So long, it just felt right to lean back in and kiss Jem again, because kissing was so much easier than figuring out the right words to say.

Me too.

Forever.

A few moments later, Jem pulled back and he was grinning. "Was that a *yes, me too, I like you a whole lot, Jem?*"

Murphy flushed. Okay—he flushed *brighter.* Because he was pretty sure all the blood in his body was currently in two places: his face and his cock.

"Yeah," he said in a strangled voice.

Jem looked very pleased with himself. "Have to say, I don't think I really appreciated the particularly romantic atmosphere of this town, back before I left."

Jem had dated, of course. He was Jem Knight. Back then, in high school, it had only been girls, even though before they'd started ninth grade, Jem had confided that he was pretty sure he liked both girls *and* boys. At the time, Murphy had wondered if Jem had been trying to tell him something—not just, *I might like boys,* but *I might like you*—but the completely friendly bro-hugs Jem had continued to give him after that confession had nipped that dream in the bud.

Murphy had gotten used to seeing Jem out, charming everyone he was with. But he'd never seemed particularly serious about any of them.

Looking back now, he could see that Jem had known he was going to leave, and he hadn't wanted anything to hold him here.

It was why, even if Jem *had* liked him like that, Murphy didn't know if anything would've ever come of it. He'd never wanted to be just another fling Jem forgot about after he'd left.

Who are you kidding? If he'd crooked his finger, you'd have come running.

Just like he had now.

Jem nudged him. "I lost you, just then."

Couldn't they just keep kissing? Even better, he should un-stick his words and just invite Jem back to his house.

If he'd been anyone else, Murphy could've done it.

But this was *Jem Knight,* and on top of that, he wanted to talk about how romantic Christmas Falls felt.

"In your defense, you weren't really looking for romance, back then," Murphy said, trying to be reasonable and not let his hope run away with itself.

Because it would.

Because it practically already had.

"I wasn't looking for romance *this* time around," Jem pointed out. He reached up and stroked Murphy's beard, which...he could do that *anytime* he wanted. "Then you came up to me in Frosty's and my entire body sat up and yowled."

"Yowled? Is this the famous Jem Knight sweet talk?" It was easier to tease him than it was to listen and take it seriously.

He was already never getting over this. If he actually con-sidered everything Jem was saying, he'd be down for the count, destroyed for life.

Jem laughed. "You're snarkier than you were when we were kids. I like it."

Murphy did not say it was a self-preservation mechanism to prevent himself from falling so deep and so hard he not only couldn't climb out, he wouldn't even want to.

"But underneath," Jem continued, still stroking, now and then finding Murphy's sensitive skin under his beard, "you're still Murphy. Sweet as hell. Too fucking adorable for your own good."

"That's what..." Murphy trailed off, barely able to speak as Jem's fingers traced his lips. Lips slightly swollen from kissing him. He cleared his throat. He *did* this. He hooked up with guys. He could be charming too. Maybe not Jem Knight brand of charming, but he *could* do better than this. "That's what all the boys say."

"What about the men?" Jem asked softly.

Because he was a man. One hundred percent man. Murphy could feel Jem's undeniable maleness under his touch.

"I don't think anyone but men are out here in this weather. You cold?" And yes, the snow had begun to pick up.

They'd have some accumulation tomorrow.

"We could always..." Jem trailed off. Waggled his eyebrows. "Find somewhere a little warmer."

And God, Murphy wanted to take him to bed. He also wanted to stay here like this forever, freezing their asses off on this bench, Jem charming him and romancing him just because he *wanted* to.

But why couldn't they have both? What if Jem's romancing continued into the bedroom?

You'll never know if you don't ask.

Murphy wasn't a guy who took many risks. He was, as Tasha always liked to say, risk-averse. But when you wanted something for as long as he'd wanted Jeremiah Knight, it turned out to be very easy to reach for it.

"Are you offering? Cause I'm asking," Murphy said.

Jem smiled but did not look surprised. Or disappointed. Or regretful, like he was going to turn Murphy down.

"Yeah," Jem said, standing and wiggling around to try to get feeling into his extremities. He looked down at Murphy. "Your place or mine?"

"Yours is closer," Murphy said.

"Eager?" Jem teased, but the glow in his eyes made it clear that Murphy wasn't the only one who wanted to get out of here and find somewhere more private.

"More than you know," Murphy said, standing too.

Jem reached out and tucked his hand into Murphy's pocket. His skin was cold against Murphy's, but he wrapped Jem's fingers with his own and squeezed hard. Trying to warm them up.

"I was surprised you weren't staying with your parents," Murphy said, searching for a subject that had nothing to do with sex.

Even though that was all he could think about, his blood racing hot and wild through his veins as they walked closer and then closer still to Jem's cottage.

Jem raised an eyebrow. "You want me to be staying with my parents right now?"

"Well, we always could've gone to my place," Murphy said.

"Yeah," Jem said, grinning, and then he moved so fast, the quickness surprising Murphy even though he knew the man was a superior athlete so it shouldn't have, and pinned Murphy to the side of his cottage, right next to the little porch.

"Yeah?"

Not sure if it was Jem's athleticism on display, the solid feel of his body pressed, chest to hip, against Murphy's own, or the heat in Jem's gaze right before he kissed him.

Jem's mouth was burning against his own, moving confidently but slowly, turning Murphy's blood to boiling lava, his brain to mush.

"Fuck," Jem said finally, stepping back. "We *almost* got inside."

"Well, uh...no time like the present?" Murphy said breathlessly, gesturing to the door, only a few feet away.

Jem grinned and the wild eagerness in it filled Murphy with determination.

Maybe they were just starting something.

Maybe this was the first and the last time.

But he'd enjoy this, *tonight*, no matter what happened after this.

"Come on, then," Jem said. There were only a few steps to the front door, and he crossed the space like it was nothing and then he unlocked it, holding the door open.

Murphy didn't need more of an invitation.

He followed him inside, and the second the door closed, Murphy pounced.

"Do you want—" Jem got out before Murphy covered his mouth with his own.

They stumbled backwards into the darkened living room.

Murphy had been in these cottages—with their similar floor plans—enough times it was easy enough to guide them to the couch.

They fell back onto it with a crash.

"Shit," Jem ground out as Murphy straddled his hips and unwound the Condors scarf from around his neck. He tackled Jem's coat next, and they both groaned, Murphy especially unsteadily, as he dug under his sweater, his cold hands hitting the rippling muscles of Jem's stomach and abs.

"Sorry," Murphy mumbled, even though he didn't feel particularly apologetic.

No. What he felt was frantic with lust.

"Don't apologize," Jem said, his words trailing away as Murphy tugged his sweater over his head.

He leaned back and got his first good look at Jem Knight—half naked and one hundred percent aroused.

"I won't," Murphy promised.

His dark hair was mussed, from Murphy's hands, and there was an equally dark dusting of hair across his broad chest and trailing down to the waistband of his jeans.

Shirtless, he was a fucking work of art, all lean, hard muscle, bunching in reaction as Murphy traced his ice-cold fingertips across all the lines and curves.

"You're gonna tease, aren't you?" Jem said, sounding agonized and also like he might *like* that.

Murphy had wanted to.

But then his gaze finally dropped from Jem's impressive chest to the equally-as-impressive erection in his jeans.

And yeah, they could go for the slow-but-inexorable-teasing sex later.

"No. Not now. Not tonight," Murphy muttered, sliding down between Jem's legs, fingers shaking as he popped open the button on his jeans and then pulled the zipper, dragging the heavy fabric down.

Jem's thighs were thick and corded with muscle, but that wasn't where Murphy's gaze snagged.

Nope. It was Jem's hard dick, cupped in his tight black briefs.

Murphy leaned down, mouthing at it through the cotton. He wasn't sure who the groan belonged to, but a second later, the fabric was gone and he got his first real taste.

Jem was salty and sweet against his tongue, just as much of a mouthful as he'd always imagined he might be.

But that was where fantasy started and where it stopped, too.

Because already the experience of sucking Jem's cock was better than any dream Murphy had ever had.

It felt real because it *was* real.

Those were Jem's hands, cradling his head. His moans, filling the air. His dick twitching against his tongue.

His undeniable smell, somehow the same even now as it had been years and years ago.

Before this, Murphy could've picked his guy out of a lineup by scent alone, but now it was stamped on his consciousness, never to be forgotten.

Jem's hips flexed against his grip, and Murphy felt his own dick grow harder when he realized just how hard Jem was fighting not to just give up and fuck his mouth.

"God, yes," Murphy insisted breathlessly, "*please.*"

His eyes met Jem's. The room was nearly dark, but he could still see Jem's intense stare like it was noon on the brightest day of the year. It bore right into him, and when he thrust up, gently at first, Murphy groaned with the perfect pressure and pleasure of it.

Palming his aching cock, he tilted his head to a better angle, inviting Jem to continue.

He didn't give a shit about the ache in his jaw—it was the sweetest ache he'd ever felt.

"God, you're so—" But Jem didn't get the rest of his words out and Murphy might never know what he was, because his hips stuttered and then tensed and he was coming in long spurts down Murphy's throat.

When Murphy finally let Jem's softening cock slip from between his lips and leaned back on his heels, Jem chuckled under his breath.

"Goddamn," Jem said, more to himself than to Murphy.

"Yeah." Murphy's voice was rough from the blowjob and from how unbelievably horny he was. Right on the edge, he was worried it would only take a touch to send him over it.

"Come 'ere," Jem said and reached down, lifting him up, and even though Murphy had inches on him, both in height and in breadth, it was hot as fuck that he could manhandle him like this.

Nobody ever did that with Murphy. They expected him to do that to *them*.

Tasha told him it was all the plaid he liked to wear.

But Jem didn't seem to have any trouble—or need any encouragement, either.

He settled Murphy on the couch and then proceeded to strip him completely naked, but not touch him anywhere where he desperately needed to be touched.

Instead, he just sat back and *looked*.

Murphy's breaths were harsh and loud in the silent room as Jem stared at him.

Did he like what he saw?

If he did, then why wasn't he touching him?

"You know," Jem said conversationally, as if Murphy hadn't just sucked his cock and wasn't right there, *this fucking close* to begging for Jem to do the same, "I never thought plaid would do it for me."

"I'm not wearing plaid," Murphy said in a strangled voice.

"No," Jem agreed. Then set a hand on Murphy's quivering thigh. So close to where he desperately needed it to be, but yet, so far, still. "But the first time I saw you in Frosty's, you were, and I wanted to do this then."

Jem leaned over his body, Murphy digging his fists into the couch, probably leaving indentions nobody would ever be able to erase, and licked up the underside of his cock, curling his tongue around the head and sucking.

Murphy swore, and of course, that was the moment Jem stopped. Let his cock slip out of his mouth.

"You're not going to come yet," Jem said and his voice was firm.

He really didn't want to. But he was kind of desperate for it.

Not just after everything that had happened tonight. Or in the last few days. Or even in the last few weeks.

Murphy's orgasm had been building for the last fifteen years.

"You're gonna let me enjoy you, before you come on my face."

"Jesus, you can't say shit like that," Murphy complained but he was already aching to do it.

To let Jem wring every bit of pleasure out of him that he could.

"Do you agree?" Jem asked, and Murphy could only nod, helplessly, as Jem dove back in, sucking him like his life depended on it.

Jem had always been fantastic at every single thing he'd set his mind to.

He'd become an incredible athlete at all the sports he tried, he was good in school, he made everybody in town like him, even when he caused trouble.

Clearly, he'd studied the art of blowjobs just as thoroughly, because Murphy had his own share of sexual experience, and he'd never been taken apart like this before, deliberately and carefully, every lick and every suck designed to drive him wild.

Several times he had to take a minute.

There was no possible way they'd ever get the impression of his fists out of the couch, and the thought of that aroused him even further.

Murphy and Jem were here, the couch could read for all eternity.

It was funny. It wasn't even the incredible dexterity of Jem's tongue, or the teasing brushes of his fingertips along his balls, but the thought of them *together*, that made him yelp and then Jem was pulling free, letting his explosive orgasm coat him just the way he'd promised.

Murphy fought the urge to squeeze his eyes shut, because he wanted to see this. He *needed* to see this.

And the view did not disappoint.

It felt like Murphy had carved into Jem's gorgeous face, *Murphy was here.*

And that felt righter than anything ever had in his thirty-plus years.

CHAPTER 9

MURPH WAS COMPLETELY FUCKING adorable—and, somehow, impossibly, inevitably so sexy Jem was barely able to restrain the yowl that wanted to escape him as he gazed over at him.

Every time their eyes met across the crowd, gathered to watch Murphy's gnome carving demonstration, Murphy flushed bright red.

He couldn't have been any clearer if he'd held up a sign that said, "I had sex with Jem Knight last night," and Jem absolutely fucking loved it.

"Now, I generally take a step back at this point. Look at it. Make sure the dude's even. That he's not listing to the side," Murphy said through the tiny microphone that Tasha had rigged up to sit near his jaw, making his voice loud and clear even to the back of the enormous crowd.

"Maybe he's drunk," someone called out.

Murphy laughed. "Maybe he is. He *is* a gnome, after all. But no," he said, leaning back after he'd finished circling the half-finished gnome, set high on a platform, already half-covered in wood shavings, "I think this little dude looks great. So next, I go through and start to add more detail. What kind of clothes is he wearing? What about a hat? I like to personalize these for every custom order, but for regular stock, I like to switch it up, but also go with whatever feels right."

"What about a Condors jersey?" someone else from the audience called out and Jem flushed. But not nearly as brightly as Murphy did—he went bright fucking red.

"I...uh...maybe," Murphy said bashfully, ducking his head a little.

"I'd ask what you did to him to make him like this," a voice next to him said, "but I think the entire crowd already knows."

Jem glanced over and saw who had to be Tasha, whom he and Murphy had gone to school with. She was now sporting fuchsia hair instead of blue, but the nose ring was the same and had been joined by a bar through her right eyebrow and a whole chain of piercings up each ear.

"Hey, Tasha," he said.

She poked him. "I know you probably think it's cute, but is he going to look back on this day and be embarrassed?"

"You're asking me? He's your friend," Jem said.

"And he's your...what, exactly? Temporary hookup?"

Jem grinned. Delighted, even though he wasn't sure why. "Tasha, is this the shovel talk? Are you really giving me the shovel talk about Murphy?"

"Of course not," she said, making a face. "I would never do that. There wouldn't be a shovel involved. I'd bury you with a fucking backhoe. So much easier. Way less sweat equity."

"And I suppose you don't think I'd deserve your sweat equity," Jem said.

"Absolutely not." She brushed an invisible piece of lint off her shoulder. "I only invest sweat equity in people who're sticking around."

Jem winced. "Ouch. Direct hit there, Tash."

She just shrugged. "I'm here to speak the truth. Even if Murph up there has got stars in his eyes."

Jem stared at the guy for a minute longer, contemplating him.

Maybe she wasn't wrong. But that didn't mean she was right either.

"What if we both have stars in our eyes?" Jem asked quietly.

He had a feeling not much surprised this woman. She'd been hard to shock in high school.

"Are you saying—"

But Jem didn't let her get the rest of her question out. He knew what she was asking, and he also knew he didn't have an answer.

Not yet, anyway.

"I don't know," he said.

"But—"

He put a hand on her arm. "I know you love him," Jem said. "And you're worried about him. But you don't have to worry about me hurting him. I'd never do it."

"Not on purpose," Tasha said a little bitterly.

"I know I hurt him leaving. That was something I had to do."

"Is that what he told you?"

Jem nodded.

"That idiot," Tasha said, with affection brimming from her tone.

"What, is that not true?"

"Oh, no, it's true." Tasha rolled her eyes. Jem wasn't sure what to make of this.

"Next time," she continued, "you get him to tell you the *whole* truth."

It was Jem's turn to be surprised. "There's a whole truth?"

"Just...promise me you'll ask him," she said.

"Of course. I want to know, I…" Jem made a face. "I don't want this to fuck him up again, I promise."

Tasha sighed and patted him on the shoulder. "Normally, I'd think you'd be a very easy person to hate, Jem Knight."

"Seriously?" Jem said.

Tasha just shrugged. "But you're actually not very hateable at all. In fact, I think I'm kinda rooting for you two crazy kids."

"That's good," Jem said, "cause I'm rooting for us, too."

In front of the crowd, Murphy was carving little bits of wood off in what seemed like a completely random way, but after a minute, he realized that Murphy was carving hair into the top of the gnome. Hair very much like the fuchsia mop currently on Tasha's head.

"He thinks he's cute," Tasha grumbled under his breath.

"I have it on good authority he is," Jem teased right back, amused at how it made her glower deeper.

Did it feel great that nobody thought he was worthy of Murphy? Not really, no, but he also understood the fierce loyalty you felt to people you loved. He'd do anything for Deacon. He *had* done anything for Deacon—when he'd come to him last year, after Jem was completely set on retirement, he'd convinced him to play one more year.

Of course, their "one more year" hadn't turned out like anyone had expected, but he'd still done it because his best friend had asked him to. Because it was important to Deacon. And funnily enough, it had become just as important to Jem, maybe even more so.

You're only fixating on it now because it didn't happen.

And while that voice was probably not wrong, it also didn't help.

"I just bet you think he's absolutely freaking adorable," Tasha retorted.

Jem forced himself not to flush. Or to reveal that before she'd arrived next to him, that was exactly what he'd been thinking.

"Do you need him for the rest of the day?" Jem asked Tasha. It might be one of the first times Jem had ever seen one of these demonstrations, but he could already tell that Murphy was winding up, with the hair he was carving mostly complete except for a few final finishing touches.

Personally, he was at a loose end for the rest of the day and there was nothing he wanted to do more than spend it with Murphy—even if they stayed totally clothed, it would still be one of the best times he'd had in any recent memory.

"Why?" Tasha asked.

Jem shot her a look.

"Okay, fine, yes, he's done for the day after this, but not because I want to let him loose with you. Only 'cause after one of these he usually needs a socializing break afterwards. Spends the rest of the day alone, in his workshop." Tasha glanced over at him, like she wasn't sure if he needed an explanation why Murphy would need something like that.

But while Tasha might have spent high school and the last fifteen years as his best friend, Jem had known him first and for just as long.

"You think he'd make an exception for me?" Jem asked, but he already knew what he hoped was the answer.

Tasha rolled her eyes. "Yes," she said simply. Sending him a look that spoke volumes.

Yes, you idiot, he'd make a shit ton of exceptions for you.

Jem didn't want to take Murphy for granted though.

"I'll ask him when he's done," Jem said, and if he wasn't mistaken, he thought he saw a glimmer of approval in Tasha's gaze.

With a quiet sigh of relief, Murphy flicked off the microphone pack tucked into the waistband of his jeans and sent Tasha an appreciative look as she stepped up, ready to distract and deflect the crowd from him.

They'd perfected this over the years—him finishing up with his demonstration and her taking over after, talking about following his company on social media, about the timeline for custom work, and pointing out what gnomes sitting around their display were still available for sale.

It took the crowds' attention at the perfect time: when he was *done* interacting with people and just needed to get away.

Murphy ducked behind one of their taller tree-shaped wooden displays and was just about to slip the pack off his waistband and undo the wire connecting it when a voice interrupted him.

"You strippin' down, honey?"

Murphy glanced up, saw Jem leaning there, looking absolutely gorgeous as he lounged against the wall, and grinned. "I didn't know you were coming today til I looked over and there you were."

They hadn't discussed today's plans this morning. Murphy had been too busy trying to make time to pull Jem's briefs off one last time to discuss minor inconveniences like plans.

But he hadn't been too busy to finally exchange numbers, either, and he'd assumed that after this was over, he'd text Jem and ask if he wanted to hang out.

He'd only promised himself that he wouldn't be so uncool as to actually put "hang out" in quotations. It turned out that once he got a taste of Jem Knight, he couldn't wait to take another bite.

Jem chuckled. "You just about swallowing your tongue was too cute to avoid."

He'd totally made it obvious by stammering and sweating and of course, flushing bright freaking red. Anyone from town who'd seen them at the pie bakeoff or at the ice skating social the night before would know exactly why he'd turned into a bumbling idiot.

He was not particularly subtle; he never had been.

"You didn't have to come," Murphy said and watched as Jem's expression flickered.

Shit. He'd said the wrong thing.

"Did you not want me to?" Jem asked, before Murphy could hurriedly add that *of course* he was thrilled that Jem had.

"No, no, no," Murphy said. "I'm glad. I'm just..."

Jem grinned at him, helping untangle him from the cord just as he was convinced he'd gotten it irrevocably caught in the buttons of his shirt.

"Adorable? Sweet? Too cute for words?" Jem teased under his breath.

"Uh," Murphy stammered.

Jem like this, in a dark green sweater, with a few days of dark scruff and that intent look in his eyes, was so potent he was impossible to resist.

Murphy didn't even want to try.

"I wanted to come," Jem said simply, then. "Wanted to see you in action, and I was pretty impressed."

"Just pretty impressed?" Murphy asked, finding his voice again.

"Okay, *seriously* impressed," Jem said. "Tasha said you normally take the afternoons off after these, but I thought...maybe you might want to play hooky with me."

"Do I want to..." Murphy trailed off, shaking his head. "You're kidding, right?"

"Am I?" Jem leaned in. It was intoxicating how quickly Jem could go from jovial to sexy-as-hell.

"I hope not," Murphy stammered. "Because yes, I definitely want to play hooky with you. Honestly, I'd want to do that any day."

"Tasha just said you usually need some alone time after these, so I wanted to make sure you didn't need that. It would be okay if you did."

Was it any wonder that high school Murphy had fallen so hard for high school Jem? He'd always been so thoughtful like that, cautious and respectful of everyone's feelings. And even now, despite being rich and famous and hugely successful, he still thought about other people first.

"No, I'm good," Murphy said. Normally, yes, he might need the downtime, but Jem didn't count as people. He'd *never* counted as people. He was in a different category entirely.

"Well, I was thinking we'd head to the White Elephant for an early dinner—unless you wanted to go to Frosty's?" Jem paused and Murphy shook his head. "Alright, then we'll head to the falls. I called Griff and begged some tickets to one of the romantic boats."

"One of the romantic boats, huh?" Murphy's voice croaked.

"You know—" Jem grinned. "The later one without all the families around."

It sounded exactly like a date. Murphy hadn't been sure if that was what they were doing—and after Jem had told him yesterday that he hadn't known what he was doing, other than he liked being with him, Murphy didn't intend to press him—but he couldn't deny the possibility filled him with a buoyant, bubbly joy.

"Sounds perfect," Murphy said.

It was the most date-like date that Murphy had ever been on. They'd shared a dinner at the White Elephant, tucked in a booth in the back, the dim light making their meal cozy. They'd laughed together like they were ten years old again, Murphy relating the good and bad and absolutely ugly about everyone they'd gone to school with. The boat ride had been just as romantic as promised, the falls lit up by the red and green lights, the chill of the air on the water making it absolutely necessary for them to cuddle together for warmth.

By the time they ended up at Jem's rental cottage again, shucking their clothes like their lives depended on getting naked as quickly as possible, sharing kisses and touches until they ended up in a sweaty, satisfied heap on Jem's bed, those bubbles of joy made him feel like he was simply floating above it, instead of lying on it.

"Comfortable?" Jem asked drowsily.

Murphy's head was pillowed by Jem's firm chest, his arm wrapped around Murphy's side, tucking him into him like he didn't want him to leave.

This was how they'd ended up last night, too, after their second round, and it was why Murphy hadn't felt, not even for a second, that Jem wanted him to go.

That the opposite was actually true.

It was true now, too.

"Never been better," Murphy said.

"Good," Jem said. He sounded very satisfied about it, even smug, like that was the only goal he had in the world.

Murphy traced the freshly healed scar on his triceps, where the surgeon had obviously gone in to make the repair to the tear Jem had endured less than two months ago.

"Didn't know you'd had surgery," Murphy said absently, as he continued pressing the still fresh-looking scar gently with his fingertips. Wishing he could make it go away. Wishing it had never happened to Jem, even though it occurring was the reason Jem was here at all, and that they were together like this.

"Not many people do," Jem said. "We thought at the time that it might help speed the recovery, make it possible for me to return by the end of the season."

Murphy heard the regret loud and clear in Jem's voice and knew that that hoped-for outcome hadn't come to pass.

"Too old, muscles not as pliant and responsive as they hoped," Jem continued, answering the question Murphy hadn't had the courage to ask.

"But it'll heal?"

"Oh sure. I'll be as strong as anything in four, five months." Jem's voice was carefully casual but Murphy could hear the darkness underneath it. The grief.

Murphy didn't want to say that was something, because at Jem's age, he certainly didn't have many years left to play, so every year he missed was hard to overcome.

But then Jem surprised him by continuing to speak. "I'm not playing next year."

Murphy twisted in Jem's arms, righting himself so he could look Jem directly in the eye.

"You're not playing next year?" Even though he was shocked, Murphy didn't miss how Jem avoided the word *retirement*, so he did as well.

There'd been a quiet sadness about Jem ever since he'd come to town. Murphy hadn't been sure if perhaps this was just the way Jem was now—after all, they hadn't even seen each other in fifteen years—but now it was becoming obvious that this was really why.

"No," Jem said, shaking his head. "I'm done. I was actually supposed to be done *last* year, but then my best friend convinced me to play with him another year. Then this happened, and I know he's retiring and I just..." He shrugged. He might pretend to others that he could be casual about it, but it was clear Jem was having difficulty hiding the pain of it around him.

Normally, that would've filled him with even more of those joyful, effervescent bubbles, but how could he feel happiness when Jem so clearly was struggling?

"This really sucks," Murphy murmured. What else was there to even say? It did suck.

"Yeah, so I came here to lick my wounds. Not really planning on letting *you* lick them, but I'm pretty happy that it's happening." Jem made an effort to waggle his eyebrows and look charming and suggestive. It didn't really work but then Murphy wasn't going to call him out on it. Not when he was clearly trying so hard.

"Me too," Murphy said. He'd always have been happy about it, but he was especially glad now. Jem needed someone in his corner. Someone he could talk to. Murphy thought of when Jem had first left town, even though they hadn't really been friends for three years at that point. He hadn't wanted to get up in the mornings. Leave his bed. He wanted to just lie there and mourn for the thing he'd known was never going to happen, but facing that it wasn't going to happen once and for all had knocked him out.

Until Tasha had come around and convinced him to put pants on and get out of bed and start living again.

She'd reminded him his whole future was ahead of him.

Maybe he could do that for Jem.

"I just know how much you love it—you *loved* it," Murphy said. "Even back when we were kids. I think you were either happiest on a football field or maybe in a huge pile of leaves, destroying some poor middle-aged guy's hard work."

A shadow crossed Jem's face.

"Now I'm that middle-aged guy," Jem said.

"I think we both are, but hey, turns out it's not such a bad place to be."

The shadow lightened, not a lot, but enough.

"Yeah, you're right. 'Course, I have no idea what the fuck this middle-aged man is gonna do with the rest of his life, now that it's not *actually* over," Jem said.

"Did you really think it was over?"

Murphy had learned the hard way that talking about your feelings was important if you wanted to pull out of this particular hole. It wasn't easy, but it *was* necessary.

Jem sighed. Murphy settled back on his chest. Maybe it would be easier for Jem if he wasn't looking at him when he said the words he'd been burying.

"For a little bit, yeah," Jem said finally. "It's why I came here, actually. Sitting at home in Charleston was hard. Even going to the practice facility, standing on the sideline at games…I thought it would help, but all I felt was worse. Like the anger and all that bitter resentment was going to eat me alive."

"So you came here," Murphy said softly.

"I needed to get away, and even here didn't sound like a bad idea, when Griff called."

"And now that you're here?" Murphy really wasn't fishing for a compliment or for a decision on whether he'd ever be open to staying.

"I…" Jem hesitated. "It's actually been good. Better than I expected."

Jem retiring next year made the whole conversation inevitably different.

Instead of being forced back to Charleston by the necessity of his job, he *could* stay. Theoretically, Jem could come here and buy a house and stay here for the rest of his life.

For the rest of your lives. Together.

Murphy cut that thought off hard and fast. Jem had made it clear they weren't making plans or writing a happy ever after. They were getting to know each other again. They were having fun. Jem didn't know what he was doing.

But part of Murphy, not even the part that wanted Jem to be his, for every day of the rest of their lives, wanted to help him. Help him find his passion, again. The way Murphy had found his own, after Jem had left town.

"Not just 'cause of me, I hope," Murphy teased softly.

He could feel Jem smile. Couldn't see it, but *knew* it was there.

"Is that your ego talking?"

"Absolutely," Murphy said with a bit more confidence than he felt.

But it had been good between them. Not just in bed, though that had been extraordinary. Everywhere else, too.

Just laughing with Jem was some of the best times he'd had.

"Really, though," Jem said, "the town's different than I remember it. I think I was just young and stupid—"

"Very young and very stupid," Murphy interrupted, poking at him a bit because he knew it would make Jem smile again. And anytime he could make Jem smile was a win.

"Hey, you tryin' to make me feel even *more* middle-aged?" Jem retorted.

"If I'm making you feel that way, can't say I don't feel the exact same 'cause we're the same age."

"Right." Jem was quiet for a minute. "Yeah, I do think I was young and stupid, and a little desperate to get away. But now? It's different. I look at this town, and I walk through it, and I don't feel like it's strangling me or smothering me. Instead, it feels sorta...reassuring, I guess. Like a warm blanket. A safety net."

Murphy didn't say anything.

He'd always loved this town, even as he'd acknowledged its downsides. The constant rounds of small-town gossip, for example. The way a lot of its inhabitants liked to think they knew best, all the time. But then, this town had also given him the chance to fly, the chance to be himself, without judgment.

Lots of small towns could be small-minded and homophobic, but Christmas Falls had never been like that.

Might be 'cause one of the sons of the town's founding family had lived forever with his "best friend" and "roommate."

Murphy could probably guess that even back then their relationship had been an open secret and as a result, the town had always tended towards acceptance instead of rejection.

"I'm still figuring this shit out," Jem continued. "But I meant what I said yesterday. I like being here. I like being here with you. And I like *you*."

"Yeah?" Murphy grinned. He shifted again, looking straight in Jem's eyes. "I like you, too. Why don't you show me just how much?"

"You sure this middle-aged man has got it?" Jem asked, stretching languorously, his naked body on full display—and the hardening cock against his thigh making it clear that however old he was, he definitely had it.

"I don't know," Murphy teased. "I think you're going to need to prove it to me."

Jem leaned in and did.

CHAPTER 10

"OH, MURPHY, I DIDN'T expect to see you here today."

Murphy glanced up from where he was arranging a few additional gnomes—tiny ones, barely a foot tall—on one of the display tables to see Jem's mom, Sophie, standing there.

He carved these small ones at night, by the light of his television, and they were always some of the bestsellers at the festival because visitors could easily tuck them into suitcases.

"Just dropping off a few extras, making sure Tasha has enough stock to last her through the weekend and the end of the arts and crafts fair," Murphy said.

He'd always been comfortable with Sophie Knight—before Jem had left town and then after, too.

She'd become a bit of an artistic mentor of sorts.

He almost greeted her the same way he always did, then suddenly, he remembered how Jem had told him she'd lectured him about getting involved with Murphy.

Yes, she'd blamed Jem and said he wasn't good enough for Murphy, but what if the opposite was actually true? What if Jem's parents really didn't approve?

He and Jem had agreed to keep whatever they were doing mostly between them—though they weren't exactly hiding it either, not if anyone who drove past the guest cottages had spotted Murphy's truck there long into the night and still there first thing in the mornings.

He'd stayed over the last few nights because it turned out they couldn't get enough of each other, and Griff had been right about one thing: he *was* at a bit of a loose end during the actual festival. Before, the whole year, he was so busy getting ready for the season, but in the season itself? He had plenty of time on his hands, if he wanted to take advantage of it.

Before, he never had, but now that Jem was here? He'd take every spare moment he could.

"Business has been good, then?" Sophie asked casually. Too casually.

Just like he knew her son, he knew Sophie too—and without the fifteen-year break, either.

"Uh, yeah, well, you know." Murphy rubbed his neck uncomfortably. He should've prepared for how he'd act when he'd see Jem's mom again. But he'd been too busy thinking about the man himself.

Jem had just texted him, less than five minutes ago, suggesting they go to the ice carving demonstration so he could, and Murphy wanted to get this line tattooed onto his heart, *get you cold so I can warm you right back up again.*

It was not even close to a mystery what Jem was gonna do to accomplish that goal, and Murphy was here for it.

But he was still flushed thinking about Jem's hands all over his body and then, *here was his mother.*

"Murphy," she said quietly. "It's okay. You don't have to be weird about it. Jem told me himself."

"Oh he did?"

She smiled. "He told me I wasn't allowed to disapprove, either."

"Ah, uh, do you?"

She sighed. "Of course not. I just worry about you."

"I'm actually worried about him," Murphy said before he could snatch the words back.

She looked surprised. Obviously not surprised that Jem was struggling—his parents must know the whole story—but that Murphy knew.

"Of course you are," she said. "I don't know why I thought he wouldn't tell you. But he would. You two were always close."

Murphy flushed. She had no idea how close they were now. Or maybe she did, and that almost made it worse, didn't it? He started to sweat under his collar.

"I only warned him off, Murphy, because I know how much this town means to you, and until now, it was a struggle to get Jem to come back here at all. Even in the offseason. I was shocked when he called me up and said he'd be here for the entire festival season. Even more shocked when he said he'd agreed to Griff's proposal."

"Things are changing for him. Not sure that has anything to do with us. Me and...uh him. Specifically."

Sophie's smile was soft and full of understanding. "I'm not sure you're right about that."

"We're not...we're just having fun. I like making him smile." *I like making him moan, too.* Murphy gave himself a firm lecture about how he wasn't supposed to be thinking about that now. Definitely not now, not in front of his mother. "Maybe lightening his mood. His burden. Just a bit."

Sophie pulled him into a hug. "I appreciate it," she said quietly into his ear. "And I know he does, too. More than he'd probably say."

Murphy didn't want to tell her that her son could definitely be vocal about what he liked.

Do not mention Jem and sex. Or how he runs his mouth during sex. Also, do not cross Go. And definitely do not collect $200.

"He's uh...well, he's said plenty." Okay, that was the best Murphy could do without word vomiting a bunch of stuff he didn't want to say to Jem's mother, and a bunch of stuff he knew Jem's mother did *not* want to hear.

She pulled back. "Good. Now when are you gonna come to dinner with him?" she asked archly.

"I...uh..." Murphy stammered. He and Jem had not discussed this. Dates at his parents' house were pretty serious, weren't they? Would they not be? He didn't know. But he was sure he wanted the invite to originate from Jem before he agreed to anything.

"I'll just suggest it to him," she said with a sly tilt to her smile.

"Ah, no. I'd just...I'd rather he ask," Murphy replied.

Sophie nodded. "I understand. But know, you're always welcome at our house. Same as always."

"Thank you, Sophie," he said and pulled her into another quick hug. "Means a lot to me."

"And you mean a lot to us." Sophie's voice sounded like a promise.

He didn't ask her if she meant her and Roger, or her and Jem, or all three of them.

But the question lingered in the back of his mind all day.

"I ran into your mom today at the arts and crafts fair," Murphy said.

Jem glanced over at him.

They were standing in Sugar Plum Park, waiting for the ice sculpture demonstration to start.

He'd suggested it because it sounded like something Murphy would specifically enjoy, and he'd discovered that unless Murphy had a reason to go to something—AKA one of his friends in town dragged him to the festival events—he mainly stayed away from them. It made sense: Murphy liked one-on-one time with his friends, and with the people he cared about, but he'd never been one for big crowds.

"Yeah?" Jem said.

He had a feeling he knew what they'd talked about, his mom and Murphy.

At dinner the other night, he'd told her and his dad that he and Murphy were "hanging out" and "getting to know each other again." The number of euphemisms he'd been forced to employ had been embarrassing, but it wasn't as embarrassing as it might have been if he'd told them the whole truth.

That they spent every night together in Jem's bed, exploring each other's bodies, and that the sex was amazing and unbelievable and he was rapidly becoming addicted to the hiccupping little gasp Murphy made just before he came.

"You could've warned me that she knew," Murphy retorted but he was grinning. "Took about ten years off my life, talking about it with her. Even in circles."

Jem wished he'd been a fly on the wall for that convo. It might've made up, at least a little, for how excruciatingly awkward his own had been.

"Guess I'm gonna have to be middle-aged alone, then," Jem teased.

"Like there wouldn't be a queue, waiting for some of that Jem Knight magic," Murphy said, still sounding more disgruntled than Jem had anticipated.

Shit. He'd made a promise that he'd treat Murphy right. No matter how long this thing between them lasted—and Jem was painfully aware it was the beginning of December, and he only had a few more weeks scheduled in town, and he didn't think a few more weeks would be nearly enough of Murphy—he didn't want to be an inconsiderate ass.

"I'm sorry. I should have mentioned to you that I told them. You shouldn't have been surprised," Jem said quietly.

Murphy nudged him. "Stop looking all woeful over there. It's fine...well, not *fine*, as it was embarrassing, but it would've been embarrassing even if I knew it was coming. Maybe I would've spent too much time agonizing over what your mom would say to me the next time we ran into each other. Or even worse, your *dad*." The corners of Murphy's lips tilted up, a mischievous glint glowing in his eyes. "Besides, you might've *planned* to tell me, but the moment we got into your house, I totally distracted you."

He had. Jem wasn't going to forget Murphy pushing him up against the door with all that surprising strength and holding him against it as he'd sucked him hard and fast, his heartbeat rabbiting wildly in his chest.

Murphy was not wrong; if he'd had a single thought in his head before that moment, it had evaporated in the unbelievable heat of Murphy's mouth.

"Yep, totally your fault," Jem joked weakly. Now he was thinking about that blowjob again, and even worse, how they might curl up tonight. His cock, which had gotten *plenty* of action this week, more action than he'd seen in ages, was somehow hard again.

Middle age, my ass.

"I was thinking," Murphy said, dropping his voice down even lower, and it scraped, rough and needy, across Jem's already strained nerves, "that tonight, after we get to your place, you should lay me back on the bed and—"

It was a little humiliating, but Jem was on the edge of his metaphorical seat, practically panting, waiting for what Murphy wanted him to do once he was on the bed.

But instead of Murphy finishing his sentence, he stopped because the crowd cheered loudly and a big guy carrying a massive chain saw and wearing goggles arrived on the stage.

"Oh look," Murphy said excitedly. "Carl's here."

"Carl?"

"Yeah, the ice carving guy," Murphy said, elbowing him in the side. "I'm real interested to see what his process is."

"I had to *convince* you to come to this," Jem reminded him, rolling his eyes.

"Yeah, and after you texted me, I might've spent an hour watching some of his videos on YouTube," Murphy said with a slight flush. "He's very talented."

Jem discovered in that moment why everyone always complained being jealous was the worst—because it felt like absolute crap. "Yeah?"

Murphy grinned and surreptitiously tucked a hand into Jem's pocket, along with his own. "Don't worry, you're *also* very talented. Do you wanna look at my YouTube history? I'm sure there's some Jem Knight videos on there somewhere."

"Better be," Jem said. But he did feel better.

Of course, the other question was how could he feel jealous if he didn't have feelings?

He liked Murphy. He'd realized that. He'd acknowledged that. He'd even told Murphy the truth about it. But that sudden flare of jealousy had felt so much more serious than mere *like*.

Okay, Jem reasoned with himself, *you like him a whole lot. You've always liked him. Since you were two toddlers, barely able to walk, you always gravitated towards each other. That's all. It's just...the sex and the like and the rest of it.*

But whatever those three things added up to, Jem didn't let himself consider the sum total.

He wasn't sure he was ready.

Murphy nudged him. "Pay attention," he hissed under his breath.

Jem looked up at where Carl was beginning to carve away the enormous ice block with the chain saw. He hadn't imagined that the guy could get so much specific shape with such a large, unwieldy tool, but he did.

"He's amazing," Murphy said in a dreamy voice. Then glanced over at Jem. The dreaminess in his look didn't fade. In fact, it seemed to grow more intense. More tender. "Don't be jealous. He's just really talented and I can always learn something new."

"You gonna become an ice carver now?" Jem didn't know how he felt about Murphy so easily identifying his jealousy. Was it that obvious? Did everyone know?

When they'd directly talked about it, after their big date, Murphy had said he didn't want the whole town to know, to be so involved with their personal business, and Jem had agreed. It wasn't like they really knew where this thing was going, and the gossip might make figuring that out even more difficult.

"Would that bother you if I did?"

Jem raised an eyebrow at Carl, then glanced back at Murphy. "You still gonna be in my bed?"

Murphy flushed in a way that made it one hundred percent clear he didn't want to be anywhere else.

"Then, no," Jem said.

"Maybe I'll work on this during the offseason," Murphy suggested as Carl finally set down the chain saw, having cut away enough that so much more than just the basic snowman shape had become clear.

It was amazing how much detail he'd managed to add with such a clunky tool. But then he switched to a small hand tool that to Jem looked quite a bit like a chisel, but longer, and a few minutes later, it was unbelievable how much progress he'd made.

"Ice is softer, easier than wood," Murphy said, but his eyes were shining. "Still, this guy is amazing."

"You wanna meet him?" Jem said, as he finished up the snowman sculpture to a loud round of applause from the gathered crowd.

Murphy shot him a look. "You're gonna use the fact that you're Jem Knight to get up there, aren't you?"

Jem just shook his head. "Actually, no," he admitted. "We're gonna use the fact that you're *Murphy Clark* to get up there."

Just as Jem had predicted, Carl had heard of Murphy, and he'd stood to the side, listening but not participating as the two carvers had a long friendly conversation about the different mediums, carving tools, and even social media presence.

When Murphy finally turned away and headed out to the edge of Sugar Plum Park, he was still glowing with excitement. "That was so freaking cool," he told Jem as they walked towards Jem's guest cottage.

"Glad you enjoyed it," Jem said, giving himself a metaphorical pat on the back. He'd seen the event on the schedule, known that even though it was right up his alley, Murphy wouldn't necessarily think to go, and decided he'd make it happen, no matter what.

It turned out it was pretty easy to bribe Murphy.

Just a hint of sex and Jem and the guy was there, eager as hell.

It was doing wonders for Jem's ego.

Or else, that was what he kept telling himself as they walked towards his cottage.

"I don't remember you being like this," Murphy said. "So sweet and thoughtful."

"I was young and an idiot, and unfortunately more than a little full of myself," Jem said dryly.

"Honestly? Even though you might've been a bit of an idiot, I liked that Jem. And I like *this* Jem," Murphy said tucking his head onto Jem's shoulder as he unlocked the front door.

Jem nearly said that he liked this Jem too—the Jem who was learning to live in this town again, to not feel stifled and hemmed in and instead understand what was so beautiful and amazing about it, and the Jem who wanted nothing more than to do right by his longest friend.

No matter what that was.

You know what it is, a voice that still sounded like Deacon's echoed in the back of his head. *You know exactly what it is.*

But before he could refocus, Murphy was shedding his boots and then taking his hand, not dragging him to the bedroom, but leading him there.

You'd go with him anywhere. You'd even go with him here, that voice added softly.

And it was true.

Jem knew it was true.

"I was trying to tell you something, before I got so distracted by the ice carving," Murphy said, sitting on the edge of the bed. His eyes were dark and intent on Jem's face as he reached over to unbutton Jem's shirt.

"What is it?" Jem was distracted, too. His internal revelations were hitting him hard and fast, and then there was the fact that they were in his bedroom, together, and Murph was undressing him, which meant that there was basically no blood whatsoever in his brain.

Murph's look turned shy. "I know we've been having a lot of fun, and I like everything we've done."

There had been a *lot* of blowjobs. Handjobs. Even one extremely memorable makeout session on the couch followed by a frantic and shockingly athletic dry hump where Jem had absolutely come his brains out.

But no they hadn't fucked, not technically, and Jem was fine with it. Either way. He wasn't lacking in spectacular orgasms.

"Tell me what you want," Jem said and leaned down, kissing him softly, slowly. Taking advantage of this less fraught moment to really enjoy the taste of Murphy and the deep, woodsy smell of him. Like pine and a crackling fire.

"Would you..." Murphy hesitated, pulling back for a second. "Would you want to do that?"

"Would I want to fuck you? Would I want you to fuck me?" Jem shook his head. "Absolutely. Either one. Or neither one. Doesn't matter to me what we do, Murph. Long as we do it together."

"God, why do you have to be so goddamn perfect?" Murphy asked roughly, and before Jem could answer that he wasn't—that if whoever Murphy had been hooking up with hadn't believed the same he wanted to meet them so he could kick their ass—Murphy leaned down and kissed him so fiercely Jem couldn't think of anything at all.

Only Murphy.

His hands trailing up Jem's chest after he pulled his shirt off, intent on mapping out every single one of his muscles, lingering at his scar, like his touch could erase the injury that had ended Jem's football career.

His mouth hot and wet under his own, leading one minute and then letting Jem lead the next.

His words, barely puffed against Jem's mouth as their breath came in uneven gasps. "Fuck me," he said, and Jem could only nod.

Anything he wanted.

Literally *anything* he wanted, Jem realized, as he dug in the drawer for the lube and condoms he'd bought—not brought with him. He'd never imagined he'd need anything like that here, but as soon as they'd had sex that first night, he'd bought them first thing the next morning.

Should've bought them after the skating social, 'cause you knew what was happening, then.

If they were being very honest—he and the Deacon-voice in his head—then he should have bought them the very first night he'd ever been here. The night he'd met Murphy and flirted with him.

Before he'd even known Murphy was Murphy.

But even then, Jem knew as he helped Murphy get naked, it wouldn't have been the same if Murphy *wasn't* Murphy. If he'd turned out to be some other random guy.

They wouldn't collapse, half giggling and half kissing, onto the bed, after finally getting Jem's jeans off.

Murphy wouldn't strain up to him like this, with all that trust in his eyes, as Jem slid his fingers down, beneath his balls, and began to rub in slow, gentle circles.

Surely it wouldn't feel the same, Jem's heart practically beating out of his chest, the first time he slid a finger into Murphy, and he squeezed his eyes shut, overcome with how right it was.

Jem didn't know he hadn't felt this way back then. *Young and idiotic* would probably cover a lot of it.

But nobody stayed the same.

Even Murphy had changed.

Was more confident. Asked for what he wanted. Pleaded. *Begged*, even, as Jem took his time fingering him open, just enjoying the slow-burning intensity of it, the heat of Murphy's body as it welcomed him so beautifully.

"Please, Jem, you gotta..." Murphy trailed off. "*Please.*"

He'd never get used to hearing Murphy's voice like that, wild and desperate, paired with the unshakeable trust in his eyes.

Or his own immense need, to give Murphy whatever he wanted.

Jem fumbled with the condom, not wanting to stop kissing Murphy even as he tried to rip the package open.

"You gotta," Murphy repeated against his lips.

Jem pulled back, and with shaking fingers, managed to roll the condom on.

Was going to turn Murphy over, but he looked at Jem, with more of that shy certainty, and shook his head. "Just like this," Murphy said softly and tilted his head up for more kisses.

Jem already knew he'd give him whatever he wanted.

But he hadn't known what it would feel like to slide into him for the first time.

The overwhelming heat of it. The need clawing its way up his spine. To go fast, to take, take, *take*, because he wasn't sure there would ever be an end to wanting him. To *needing* him.

He felt like he was inching closer to the precipice, and he'd never been this close, and he couldn't see over the edge. He should be terrified of what lay beneath. If it would hurt him. Maybe even kill him.

But all he felt was exhilarated.

"More, *more*," Murphy begged, and Jem thought, before his whole brain fizzled out, in a rush of pleasure, that maybe Murphy was feeling the same.

Jem's fingers dropped to Murphy's knee, caressing it, loving the strength of it and also the way he always trembled when Jem touched him. Lifted him up a little higher, trying to find a better angle, and Murphy wailed.

The sounds he was making, the pleasure on his face, the intensity of heat pressing around him, the very thought that he was *inside* Murphy as close as he could possibly get, wrenched Jem closer than he wanted to his orgasm.

But first, he wanted—no, he *needed*—Murphy to get there. He wanted to feel him clench around him. He wanted to feel Murphy lose all his composure.

He reached down, and Murphy tensed when he circled his cock, hard and leaking against his palm, with his hand.

"Yeah, baby," Jem encouraged as Murphy leaned into it, like he couldn't get enough.

Jem liked sex well enough. Most people did.

But this was so far beyond sex it felt as if he'd never even done this before.

Murphy cupped his head with his hand and dug his fingertips into Jem's hair, pulling him down.

They kissed, and Murphy clenched around him, come spurting out of his cock between them.

Murphy's orgasm pulled Jem right into his own, and that was it, he groaned and made one last thrust before letting the pleasure overtake him.

He vaguely remembered pulling out, flopping down on the bed next to Murphy, and certainly not giving a shit how fucked up the bedding got.

Murphy curled into him, a soft, sweet smile on his face.

"That was…" He trailed off.

Turned out the bottom of the cliff was just fine. It felt like Murphy's shoulder. Tasted just like his mouth, as he leaned in and kissed him.

Usually Jem hated change.

"Yeah," Jem said, because even though this felt good—*great*, honestly—he didn't have any idea what the fuck he was doing.

He'd never felt like this before. Not about anyone.

"The best ever?" Jem confessed.

Murphy's eyes widened. "Yeah?"

"Yeah," Jem said.

He might not be able to vocalize how he was feeling. He might not have words for the emotions surging through him. But he also wasn't going to lie to this man either.

His man.

Especially when he still didn't know what the hell he was going to do about it.

Don't be extra stupid, the Deacon-voice lectured in the back of his head. *You don't have to do anything about it. You just have to feel it.*

But that wasn't true either, was it?

"We should clean up," Murphy said.

But neither of them moved. Except, in Jem's case, to get even closer. To wrap an arm around Murphy and tug him insistently into what he was beginning to think of as "his spot"—his head on Jem's pectoral muscle, his arm draped across his stomach.

Maybe Deacon wasn't wrong, after all.

CHAPTER 11

"You sound...different," Deacon said after Jem answered the phone.

Deacon sounded puzzled by this fact. Which...that tracked, because the Deacon in his head was definitely not the *actual* Deacon, who had no idea what was going on with Murphy.

"Yeah?" Jem asked, settling out on the chair on the tiny porch of his cottage.

He could see Felix getting in his car the next cottage over and waved at him from a distance. They hadn't had much time to chat since the new employee at the tree farm had come over a few nights back, freaking out about his boss. The cookies he'd brought had gone down easy, and Jem thought he'd given the guy some decent advice. Hopefully things would work out for Bruce and him, at least as well as they were working out for Murphy and him.

Jem had texted Deacon and told him to call after he got to the team hotel, because he hadn't felt right texting his best friend to tell him about Murphy.

Murphy was worth more than just a text.

He was worth a whole freaking phone call.

"Happier, almost. Lighter, for sure," Deacon said.

Jem felt a flare of guilt. He was happier here than he'd been in a long time but the news coming out of Charleston had never been worse.

What was going on there? He'd considered leaving, but after he'd texted the suggestion to Deacon, he'd insisted there was no reason for Jem to cut his Christmas Falls visit short.

"You want to talk about it?" Jem asked.

Deacon made a scoffing noise. "Hell no. That's not why I called you. There's nothing you can do." He paused. "So, you gonna tell me why you're so happy? I know that's why you wanted me to call you. Something's up."

Jem chuckled. "Let a guy answer your freaking question before you start interrogating him."

"Well, what is it?" Deacon demanded. "Last time we talked, I thought I was gonna have to go MIA and come there myself. Drag you out of the pity party you were throwing for yourself."

"Unfair," Jem retorted.

"Maybe. But you tryin' to tell me you didn't drag yourself out of it?"

"Sort of." Jem picked at a loose thread on the knee of his jeans. "Me and someone else, yeah."

"Ah, *someone else.* That's why you wanted me to call you. You, Jeremiah Knight, met someone. It's about fucking time."

"Deac," Jem warned.

"You're more painfully single than I've ever been, and that's saying something."

"Well, uh...not anymore," Jem said.

He and Murph hadn't talked about exactly what was happening between them—but it wasn't very hard to figure out either. When you spent every waking moment you could with someone and they made you smile and laugh like it was going out of style and you wanted them there at night, not necessarily to get naked, but just to feel their big, warm body pressed up against yours?

That was not a casual hookup.

Add in the way he'd always felt about Murphy and how it was now evolving into something both similar and utterly different than how he'd felt about him when they were kids, and Jem was not stupid.

They were heading into a serious place.

It wasn't that Jem was *against* love. It was that he was thirty-three-years old, and he'd never felt it before. Had kind of begun to assume that maybe love, romantic love in the way everyone talked about and sang about and wrote about was just not for him.

Wrong again, bucko.

Having one Deacon in his head was trouble enough—but right now he apparently had two of them.

Make-believe Deacon and also real Deacon.

"You gonna tell me about them?" Deacon asked archly. "Or are you just gonna sit there in moony silence, contemplating just how amazing and wonderful and breathtaking they are?"

Jem rolled his eyes. "His name is Murphy, and we used to be friends, way back before I left town. And I was *not* doing any of those things." Except he kinda was.

"Don't front with me," Deacon said. "I'm surrounded by happy couples. That's what they *do*. So, Murphy, huh? That's what Mr. Lumberjack's name is."

Of course Deacon had remembered Mr. Lumberjack. After all, he *had* mentioned him the last time they'd actually talked.

"So I guess he didn't hate you very much after all," Deacon continued, in a teasing voice. "Or else the mighty Knight slayed that dragon."

"That's not funny."

"Disagree. It's fucking hilarious."

"No, he did not hate me," Jem said with as much dignity as he could muster.

"I kinda figured," Deacon said. "So you movin' there now? Gonna buy a house with a white picket fence and learn to love Christmas again?" He said it jokingly, but Jem could hear the serious question underneath the lightheartedness.

"I don't know," Jem said slowly. "Nice thing about being rich. You can kinda do whatever the fuck you want. Whenever you want. I could live here sometimes. I could still live in Charleston. Hard to say, when I don't know what I'm doing next."

"But it's serious enough you're thinking about it?" Deacon asked, but they both knew it was a rhetorical question.

Deacon knew him too well to not realize it was serious.

Not if the guy in Jem's life rated a phone call to tell Deacon about him.

"I guess so, yeah," Jem said.

"Mr. Lumberjack must be something else," Deacon mused.

"Yeah," Jem repeated. Cleared his throat when he realized just how lovestruck he'd sounded just then.

Deacon laughed. "It's cool, man. I'm happy for you. I said it before—you've been alone for too long."

"I dated," Jem said defensively. Except that wasn't really true, was it?

He'd tried, for a long time, to find someone he clicked with, but it had never happened. And after so long a time trying, it had started to seem pointless. It had been easier to just stop.

"Not seriously," Deacon reminded him.

"Okay, fine, not seriously," Jem said. "But it's serious now."

"If I was Carter, I'd tell you that you were just waiting to meet the right person. Or I guess in your case, to meet the right person *again*."

"It wasn't like that before, between us. We were kids," Jem reminded him.

"Uh-huh," Deacon said, laughing. "Sure. You tryin' to tell me he didn't have a huge-ass crush on you? *You*? Jeremiah Knight, hero of Christmas Falls?"

"Ugh, I hate you," Jem said. "It's bad enough to be the center of attention here without your additional commentary added to it."

"You've always pretended like you're not something special," Deacon said bluntly. "But you are. You've got something to say and something to share. Even if it's not on the football field."

"I don't know." Jem knew how uncertain he sounded.

"What about last year? When you gave that talk at the rookie symposium? Or when you took Beck under your wing?"

"That wasn't entirely me," Jem said uncomfortably.

Except that yeah, it had been his idea. He'd protected the rookies, he'd *always* protected the rookies, because he knew how jarring and difficult the transition to the NFL was, and he hadn't wanted any of them to struggle the way he'd struggled.

So he'd fought for them, fought the way he'd always hoped someone would've fought for him, way back when.

"I'm just sayin'," Deacon pointed out. "You were great at that. You *are* great at that."

"Thanks, man," Jem said. He hesitated. "But that's not a career."

"It's not?" Deacon questioned.

Jem considered this. Couldn't believe he hadn't necessarily thought of it before now, because yes, writing that presentation he'd given at the rookie symposium last year had taken him a full month. And he'd been more into it than he'd been forever. But then the season had started, and that had taken all his time and energy. He'd not necessarily forgotten about what he'd done, but it had been superseded by something more important: playing football.

But that part of his life was done and over, now.

"I'm just saying," Deacon said, "you *just* told me that you have all this money. Which, right, we all do. But you've saved.

You weren't an extravagant asshole. You don't have to *work* again. But that doesn't mean you can't do something." He paused. "So, *do* something, Jem. You always knew you weren't going to be a football player forever."

Yeah, he'd known. But knowing it and *understanding it* were two entirely different things.

Maybe his life wasn't over, but that still didn't mean he knew what the fuck he was doing.

"I hate you," Jem said in a way that he knew made it clear the exact opposite was actually true.

"I know," Deacon said.

"How long have you been waiting to suggest that to me?"

Because now that Jem looked back, he could see the seeds of it.

"Until you were ready to listen," Deacon said.

He didn't have to say Jem hadn't been ready before. He knew he hadn't been. The last time they'd talked, when Deacon had told him about his own retirement plans, he'd still been in deep mourning for what could've been.

Deacon was right; he hadn't been ready to hear what else he could do with his life, even a few weeks back.

But he'd begun to come out of the fog. Had Murphy helped? Yeah, because he'd shown him his life wasn't over. The rest of the process, him working through his feelings and coming to terms with them, accepting them and internalizing them, was a different but no less integral part of moving on—and he was making that effort himself.

Each day he felt a little lighter.

"I was ready now, then?" Jem asked archly.

"Sure seemed like it," Deacon teased. "Mr. Lumberjack might have something to do with that."

"His name is Murphy."

"Sure." And Jem knew he'd probably be Mr. Lumberjack to Deacon forever. Probably when the two of them met—and he knew that was not an *if* but a *when*, now—Deacon would call him Mr. Lumberjack.

"Have to say though," Deacon continued, "I'm happy for you."

"Thanks, Deac," Jem said. "When are we gonna have this conversation about *you*?"

Jem could hear Deacon freeze on the other side of the line.

"I don't know what you mean," he said.

But they both knew what Jem was saying. What he was referring to.

"You're retiring, Deac," Jem reminded him. "He's not gonna be your boss anymore."

"Doesn't mean—" Deacon stopped abruptly. "We're still not talking about this."

"But we will someday," Jem said.

"Someday," Deacon agreed.

"Someday *soon*," Jem added.

Jem might not be able to see Deacon roll his eyes, but he knew his friend well enough to know that was exactly what was happening.

"I don't know about that," Deacon said.

But Jem did, because he knew all of Deacon's moods. All the different inflections of his voice. And his friend didn't sound nearly as certain as he once had.

Something was happening between Deacon and the owner of the Condors, even if he tried to pretend it wasn't. And Jem was ecstatic about it. It was about goddamn time.

He heard Murphy's truck before he saw it come around the bend.

"Hey, Deac, I gotta go," Jem said.

"Your boy's here," Deacon said reasonably. Like he just had to hear the change in Jem's voice to know.

"Yeah," Jem said.

Was Murphy *his boy*? Well, he was his *something*.

"What are you two up to tonight?" Deacon asked. "Building snowmen? Cutting down Christmas trees? Stringing them with lights? Caroling? Covering yourselves in glue and rolling around in glitter?"

"No, no, no, and *no*," Jem said, laughing. "It's actually the first night of this big holiday light tour. A ton of homeowners get really into it, decorating their houses, and you can take these sleighs around the participating streets."

"I never thought you'd sound that excited about holiday lights," Deacon said gently.

"Me neither," Jem admitted. "Anyway, I'm dragging Murph along, because I've learned judging things without him around isn't nearly as much fun as doing it with him."

"And 'cause you don't want to let him out of your sight."

"Probably," Jem said.

"'Cause you love him," Deacon said very reasonably. Like this was the obvious conclusion to come to.

And…maybe it was.

Jem watched as Murphy parked his truck and got out, walking towards him.

It was funny how the mischievous but quiet kid merged now in his mind with the sexy-as-hell mountain of a man he'd become.

He'd loved Murphy then, in the purely platonic way of children. But the way he loved Murphy now was different.

Because he was pretty sure now that Deacon was right.

He loved Murphy.

"Yeah," Jem said, his voice cracking a bit.

"Good. Now, have fun. Use protection. Don't do anything stupid."

Murphy stopped just short of the porch stairs, leaning against them. He was back in plaid, his dark beard gleaming in the setting sun.

"Ditto to you," Jem retorted. "Be safe tomorrow and good luck."

"Thanks," Deacon said, and hung up.

"Sorry," Jem said to Murphy, who was gazing at him with an intent smile full of warmth and trust and...if Jem wasn't reading this wrong...*love*.

"No problem," Murphy said. He leaned in and Jem was already up on his feet kissing Murphy across the railing.

"That was Deacon," Jem said when they finally pulled back, a bit breathless.

"Yeah?"

"Yeah," Jem said. He shot Murphy a look. "I told him about you. About us."

Murphy grinned. "Us?"

Jem reached out and took Murphy's hand and squeezed it. "Pretty sure there's an *us*, Murph. Or at least I'm hoping that's what there is."

"Pretty sure there is," Murphy said, and then they were kissing again, Murphy barely breaking contact with his lips as he moved onto the porch and then pressed Jem right back against the door.

"I don't want to go tonight," Jem admitted when Murphy finally raised his head. "Wanna stay here, with you." The confession felt intimate. Like he was saying more than he really was.

"We gotta, though," Murphy pointed out regretfully. "After though, that's all us. *Just* us."

"Deal," Jem said.

Murphy was seriously beginning to question the intelligence of telling Jem, when they'd first started this...well, he couldn't call it a hookup, could he, because it was obviously so much more than that...*us*, that he'd wanted to keep it under wraps. At least for now.

That meant, they were both in the back seat of the sleigh, being pulled towards the first street of the tour, but it also meant they couldn't hold hands, and cuddling up next to Jem's warm body was a no-go, not unless he wanted everyone wandering around the streets to spot them and start talking.

Okay, not *start* talking, but *keep* talking.

"Glad it's not so cold tonight," Jem said as he tucked the blanket more securely around his waist. Used the excuse to reach out and briefly squeeze Murphy's knee.

"Yeah," Murphy agreed. Though if it had been, maybe he'd have given in and just said, *come here and let's keep each other warm, fuck all this noise from the town.*

"It was good to talk to Deacon," Jem said a minute later.

"You said you told him about us." Murphy knew Deacon was Jem's best friend, whom he'd played with in the NFL for years. He knew, too, that Deacon was retiring after this year, which had been part of Jem's difficulty in reconciling himself to leaving football.

He wouldn't ever play with his best friend again.

"Yeah, and we talked about me being here. Uh, and what I want to do in the future."

Murphy knew something about best friends and how they knew you better than you knew yourself.

Thank you, Tasha.

"He had an idea, didn't he?"

Jem grinned. "How'd you guess?"

"Best friends. They're always the interfering sort. Usually in a good way. Tasha always knows what I should do before I do it. Sometimes she pulls me aside and just *tells* me, but sometimes she waits until I've stumbled onto it and it's my idea before she admits she knew it all along."

"It's annoying, isn't it? But kinda nice, too," Jem said thoughtfully.

"You gonna tell me what he suggested?"

"Last year I gave a talk or sort of a presentation, at the rookie symposium."

"Rookie symposium?"

"Yeah. So, this is a new thing they're trying, the last few years, with all the rookies in the NFL. It started as just a single presentation, and then it kept expanding. It's *still* not enough, not at all, in my opinion, but it's better than nothing. Which is what they had before."

"A mentor, huh?" Murphy tilted his head, considering this. Knowing immediately how well that position would suit Jem.

"We treat rookies like shit. Like they already know everything, and they don't know *anything*," Jem said bluntly.

"You'd be great at that."

"Deacon thought so. I don't know what it means or what I'd do, but it's a direction, something to *do*, and I didn't have that yesterday so..."

Murphy nudged him. "You don't have to have it all figured out, you know?"

"I'm thirty-three," Jem said dryly.

"And transitioning to a new career. Hey, unlike most people who do that, you don't have to worry about supporting yourself."

"True," Jem said. "So, what did *you* do today?"

"Worked on your gnome, actually." Had gotten about halfway done and had seriously considered throwing it out and starting over, but then Tasha had walked in and burst into tears and since she wasn't much for waterworks, he'd known that even if the whole idea ended up being nothing that Jem wanted, he hadn't gone in the wrong direction after all.

He'd put himself out there.

He'd made his feelings clear.

Unlike high school, when he'd chosen to fade from Jem's life instead of figuring out if he could ever feel the same as Murphy did.

Of course, he still had to *give* Jem the gnome, but he decided that carving it at all was taking a pretty damn big step.

"Oh yeah?" Jem sounded excited. "When can I see?"

"When it's done." *And when I find the courage to show you.*

"Can't wait." Jem reached over and squeezed his knee again, saying something shockingly eloquent with his eyes as he did so.

Something like, *I know I'm gonna love it.*

Or, *I wish we could get out of here and I could show you.*

Maybe, *skin to skin, that's how I want to be with you.*

Murphy wanted that too, but this was nicer than he'd thought.

The sleigh pulled up to the first street. "You two wanna get out, or I can drive down?"

Jem glanced over at Murphy. "What do you think? Sleigh or foot?"

"Let's walk," Murphy said. Maybe he could surreptitiously tuck his hand into Jem's pocket.

You need to believe he's not gonna just bail on you again. That it won't be the same as before.

Maybe if he could really believe those two things, he wouldn't care anymore if everyone in town knew the truth.

"Yeah, this is nice," Jem said, as they took in the first house.

"You makin' notes, or do you want me to?" The whole purpose of touring the houses the first night of the tour was so Jem could judge them and pick a top five. The committee would combine Jem's scores with the popular vote, and that would determine the winners.

"What kind of liaison are you, if I gotta keep my own notes?" Jem teased, whipping out a notebook from his coat pocket. He waved it in front of Murphy. "I got this, babe."

"Yeah," Murphy retorted weakly, knees still wobbly from Jem's casual *babe*." Griff would have my head if I didn't make sure to liaison you properly."

Jem waggled his eyebrows. "If you're making promises, you'd better make good on them later. I want to be *properly* liasioned."

Murphy flushed. "You got it."

"Now, this first house..." Jem eyed the candy canes lining the driveway, matching with the red and white lights covering the whole house and the gigantic gingerbread man inflatable in the yard. "I think full points for theme."

"Does it really have a theme, though?"

"It's a food theme, yeah?" Jem said, scribbling down in his notebook.

Murphy considered. "Maybe a gingerbread house theme?"

"Well, we'll dock them a point or two for execution," Jem said.

Each house they passed seemed more fantastically decorated than the last.

There was a house exclusively decorated in holly outlined in lights, with a whole forest of light trees in the front yard. A bungalow turned into an elves' workshop.

Two themed houses – the Grinch and the Nightmare Before Christmas.

And finally, they walked up to the last house on the block.

Jem glanced up and Murphy was standing close enough to him he felt him freeze in place.

"That's neat," Murphy said, taking in the lines of red and orange lights and the mini football field, complete with football, all created with mini white lights. The crowning achievement was an enormous Condors logo, created entirely from LED lights, wings spreading out across the top edge of the roof.

Jem didn't say anything, just stared at the house.

"And also smart branding," Murphy continued, because he wasn't quite sure how to interpret Jem's total silence. "Clearly trying to appeal to the judge here. If they were attempting to win the popular vote, they'd have done it all up in blue and orange, for the Bears."

Jem still said nothing.

"Or maybe they're just big fans." Murphy chuckled awkwardly. Why didn't Jem say anything? Why was he staring at the house like it was going to reach out and grab him by the throat and—

Abruptly Jem turned and walked away, moving so fast Murphy had to practically jog to catch up with him.

"Jem, hey, wait up!" Murphy called out.

Jem pulled up, right by the stop sign.

He was breathing heavily, his face a hard mask under the streetlight.

"Hey, you okay?" Murphy asked, putting a hand on his arm.

Jem finally glanced over at him. Cracks were showing in the mask, and Murphy could see the raw pain in him—and the uncertainty. He looked like he was debating with himself.

"Is this all I'm ever gonna be?" Jem asked, in a raw voice.

"All you're ever gonna be?" Murphy didn't think he understood what he meant. He was Jeremiah Knight. Hometown hero. The guy everyone had always liked. The guy who'd come back here to Christmas Falls, just because the town had needed him.

"All I'm ever gonna be is a football player." His chest rose and fell rapidly. Like he was this close to losing control. "To everyone, that's all I'm gonna be. Some big dumb football player."

"You're not dumb. And as for big..." Murphy took a risk. "I'm bigger than you."

Jem shot him a look. A much less angry look. "If you think you're gonna distract me from this with sex."

"Honest to God, I wasn't." Though Murphy didn't think that sounded like such a bad idea. And yet, it was, because he knew, better than anyone else, that sex wouldn't address more than the surface-level frustration. It wouldn't fix Jem, deep inside, where he needed to heal the most.

"Okay," Jem said uncertainly.

Murphy put his hands on Jem's shoulders. Decided he didn't care who was watching, and curled his fingers into his jacket, tugging Jem closer, until they were practically embracing, Jem looking at him with wide, serious eyes.

"You're so much more than that. It's what you *did,* as a job, Jem. Yeah, you might've been a football player for most of your life. But more than that, more than anything, you're *Jem*. You're a friend. A loyal, kind, generous friend. Who gives a shit about people. Who, even though he didn't like this town when he left it, came back because he realized he was needed. And was willing to change his mind about it. You're so much more than just the sum of your parts. Look at what your best friend thought you should do—*mentor* these kids, who don't know their head from their ass. Do you think someone who was just a football player, who could only ever play football, would be able or *willing* to do that? Wanting to do that?"

At the end of his rant, it was actually Murphy's breath that was ragged.

Jem didn't say anything for a minute. Like he was mentally repeating everything Murphy had said, and he was slowly, deliberately, absorbing each and every word.

"Well, when you decide to offer your opinion, Murph, you really offer your opinion," Jem said softly, giving him a tremulous smile.

Even if Jem never loved him the way Murphy loved Jem, he could never see these last few weeks—and whatever they shared in the future—as a waste because he'd done this. He'd made Jem stop and reconsider. He'd offered him a different opinion. A window into the way Murphy saw him.

The way Murphy had *always* seen him.

"You needed to hear it," Murphy said. "Sometimes we can get lost in our own heads and we don't see things right."

Jem reached up and brushed a kiss across Murphy's bearded cheek. "You're right," he said wryly. "I can't say I'm necessarily okay. Thought I was more okay than I had been. I was definitely not expecting that to hit me the way it did, but then we stopped at that house, and it was just like a ton of bricks."

"Everything's changing," Murphy reminded him. "It's okay to not be okay."

Jem chuckled. "It kinda sucks, though." He tucked himself in a little closer to Murphy and Murphy slid an arm around his shoulders. "Not all of it, though."

"Yeah?"

"Some parts are really freaking great," Jem admitted.

Murphy knew what he was talking about. But he was just needy enough to ask. "Which parts, then?"

Jem laughed, and the happiness Murphy had begun to hear more and more recently was back in spades, glowing in his eyes. "Just one part, actually. You, Murph. It's always you."

Good. Cause it's always been you too, Jem.

Murphy didn't say it because it still seemed too early, and there was the matter of that old crush he still hadn't quite managed to tell Jem about, but he hoped that if Jem looked deep into his eyes, he might see the truth there.

"I'm happy about it, too," Murphy said.

An understatement.

"Should we see the next neighborhood?" Jem asked.

"I guess we have to," Murphy admitted. Even though, even more than he had before, he wanted to curl up, naked, with this man.

Not because sex would distract Jem from his pain.

But because he wanted to give Jem all the love he could. Maybe Jem could absorb it through osmosis, and if it helped alleviate even a fraction of Jem's sadness, it would all be worth it.

"Griff would kill us if we skipped out," Jem reasoned.

"Come on, there's only three neighborhoods of houses left," Murphy said, trying for optimism.

Jem laughed. "Only three, huh? Then what?"

Murphy curled his fingers into Jem's. "Anything you want," he said.

And meant every word.

Chapter 12

"Come on," Jem said breathlessly, pushing Murphy back against the shower wall.

In the last week, they'd started spending time not just at Jem's guest cottage, but at Murphy's small house, too.

The first time Jem had seen it, after they'd finished the house tour, he'd shot Murphy a look and said, "And why have we been spending every freaking night at *my* place, when you have this incredible shower that we could have shared?"

It wasn't like Jem's shower back in Charleston was any different. It was just as large. Filled with steam the same way.

But there was one very important difference between Jem's shower in Charleston and Murphy's shower here in Christmas Falls: it was full of Murphy.

Naked, eager Murphy.

Jem pushed Murphy back against the tile, ignoring his yelp of surprise at the cold surface, one hand stroking the hair on his chest, the other drifting lower, to where Murphy was hard and ready for him.

"Shit," Jem said, aware of how completely not eloquent he was right now.

"We're supposed to be getting ready to go to the beer and cider thingy," Murphy said breathlessly as Jem's fingers stroked him.

"Yeah, I know," Jem said. Then leaned forward and kissed him hard.

It wasn't his fault he couldn't get enough of the man.

The man he loved.

That particular title felt a little more comfortable a week into his realization.

He'd begun to not only come to terms with it, but to enjoy it.

To practically *revel* in it

Which was why even more now than before, Jem couldn't get enough of Murphy—even to the point of probably making them very late for the kickoff of the beer and cider festival.

Murphy groaned into his mouth as Jem pressed his own hardening cock against his thigh, rubbing it along the tense muscle there.

They could just get off like this, but it would be slower. Achingly slower. Hot, like that, undoubtedly, but they were probably already running behind, after Jem had climbed on top of Murphy this morning and woken him up with a long, lazy makeout session.

Murphy had claimed they didn't have time for anything else, but then Jem cornered him in the shower—plenty big enough for two of them—and had decided it was a good idea to change his mind.

It would be far quicker, Jem thought sluggishly, to do things this way. Quicker, and even better.

He knelt, Murphy's head hitting the back of the tile wall as he sucked him down.

The problem was yes, *theoretically*, it would absolutely be faster to get them both off this way, Jem working his own cock, arousal pounding relentlessly through his veins as he sucked Murphy off, but the reality was a different story entirely.

As soon as the flavor that was totally, uniquely Murphy hit his tongue, it was like a switch flipped in Jem's head, and suddenly speed was the last thing on his mind.

Instead, he felt compelled to undo Murphy one long, slow suck at a time, teasing his cock with his tongue, playing with his balls until he was begging and pleading for Jem to finish him off.

But even then Jem didn't want to give in. Didn't want it to be over, not quite yet.

He wasn't ready to let go.

Not even when he tucked a finger wet with spit into Murphy's body, loving the way it tensed and bowed at the double onslaught of pleasure.

Jem was right on the edge himself, barely touching himself anymore because Murphy's pleasure was so intoxicating it was like an echo in his own blood. Making it pulse hard and fast as he finally gave in and took them both over.

"God," Murphy cried out, pulsing into Jem's mouth and Jem groaned around his cock, his own orgasm overtaking him.

Jem flopped back against the wall. "My knees are fucking shot," he said, but he was laughing. Couldn't help himself.

"Maybe we should get you a cushion. I'm sure they make waterproof cushions," Murphy teased, lifting him to his feet. "You're gonna get us in serious shit with Griff if we're late *again*. We were already ten minutes late to the wine tasting earlier this week."

Jem raised an eyebrow, soaping up as Murphy began to wash his hair. "And then there was the fact we ducked out after only being there for forty minutes."

"Hey, not our fault we're not into wine."

"I don't think the wine was the issue. Maybe it had something to do with the fact your hand was on my thigh under the table. My *upper* thigh."

Murphy flushed, and it felt good to know, deep down, that Jem wasn't the only one who was stuck in this incandescently happy bubble. Not even remotely the only one who couldn't keep his hands to himself.

Thirty minutes later they were dressed and pulling into the parking lot adjacent to Sugar Plum Park.

Marlene shot Jem a look across the plaza. It was full of tents, every one of them strung with holiday lights, with heaters dotted every so often.

"I see you finally made it," she said, her voice a little frosty. "I ended up opening the festival myself."

"We're only…" Jem glanced down at his watch. "Uh…"

"Forty-five minutes late?" Marlene asked, arching her eyebrow.

So much for hoping that Griff wouldn't hear about this. He would. Marlene, who was normally a very reasonable person, looked incredibly frustrated.

"Sorry. Got…uh…tied up." Now *that* was a thought.

Marlene rolled her eyes. "Right. Of course you did."

It was probably foolish to think they could keep this under wraps. It was obvious to Jem that everyone either knew or had guessed.

But Murphy continued to maintain that he didn't want to be public about their relationship. Not yet, anyway, he'd said, just as they were driving into town this morning.

Jem hadn't gone down on one knee and promised to spend the rest of his life here, but he'd certainly made it clear that this wasn't a fling. He had feelings. He knew Murphy did too. Why couldn't they stop sneaking around?

He didn't understand it, but he was also not willing to jeopardize what they had by pushing Murphy too hard, too fast.

"Shouldn't have taken that shower," Murphy said as soon as she walked off.

Jem shot him a look. "Are you saying you didn't enjoy that?"

He didn't even have to ask. Murphy was freaking glowing. They both were.

Maybe that was the problem, why Jem kept trying to drag Murphy to where they could be alone and keep him there. Because when they were out here like this, in public, Murphy insisted on keeping his distance.

And distance was the last thing on Jem's mind.

"You know I did," Murphy said, a confused wrinkle appearing between his dark eyebrows. "I think my enthusiasm for you on your knees is well documented."

"Might not hurt to double check though," Jem teased. "Later?"

Murphy rolled his eyes, but Jem wasn't fooled. He knew Murph was just as into it as he was.

If only he was as into this as you are. If he was, he'd be okay with people knowing. Especially considering everyone's already freaking guessed.

It was hard to dismiss that voice, especially because it didn't sound anything like Deacon's.

Instead it sounded like the worst version of himself, buried in the back of his mind, unsure and uncertain and full of doubts.

Not about Murphy.

But about himself.

"Come on," Murphy said, "let's get a beer."

"It's not even noon," Jem teased.

"A cider then. What else do you have going on today?"

"I was gonna talk to my agent later, but maybe that talk'll go better if I've had something to drink," Jem said with a dark chuckle.

"Yeah?" Murphy asked as they stopped by the front entrance, letting the guy checking IDs put their bracelets on, indicating they were of-age.

"Talk about depressing," Jem said, instead of answering Murph's question. "Apparently we don't even get carded anymore. Do we really look that old?"

Murphy smacked him in the side. "You're *Jem Knight.* Everyone knows you and knows you're practically ancient. And I'm with you, so I'm getting lumped in with you. Thanks for that, by the way."

Jem's good mood, which had filled him this morning with such effervescent bubbles, was slowly dribbling out. He wanted to reach out and grab it back, but how could you find something you couldn't see and couldn't touch?

He made a face as they approached one of the cider tasting booths.

"Hey, you want apple or pear? Or what about this spiced cider? That could be good." Murphy was babbling about cider, and Jem was suddenly struck with the intense desire to reach over and kiss him right here. In front of the crowds milling around and all the volunteers at the Beer Fest. But he didn't, because what he wanted, really truly wanted, was for *Murphy* to be the one to decide they didn't have to pretend they were just friends any longer.

"I don't really care," Jem said. "The spiced one sounds fine." He dropped two of the wooden coins Marlene had given him into Murphy's palm. "I'm gonna go grab us a table." Murphy nodded.

He settled down at an empty table on the outskirts. Smiled back at a few kids who were staring at him with huge eyes, like they'd just recognized him. He was sure that before they left, they'd come up for an autograph and probably a selfie, too.

"So, what do you need to talk to your agent about?" Murphy said as he set down their glasses of cider and slid onto the wooden bench.

"Uh well, I'm gonna talk to him about this rookie mentorship idea I have. Programs I want to start."

"He's not gonna be happy about it?" Murphy asked, frowning. "Wouldn't he be glad you're doing something with your life after you retire?"

"Yeah, he will, but I think he was hoping I'd do something more...lucrative? Go on TV? Sign a big broadcasting contract? Start a podcast? Be more present in the public eye instead of working behind the scenes?"

"You'd hate all those things," Murphy said flatly.

"Yeah, I would. He knows that too, 'cause we've talked about it, but I think he's still holding out hope."

"And you're gonna kill that last little bit, aren't you?"

Jem nodded. "But I think he knows it's coming."

"If he's met you, he will," Murphy said.

"Yeah, he knows," Jem said, chuckling. He sipped his cider. "This is pretty good, actually."

"I had them mix the spiced cider with some of the pear cider. I tried a sample, and the cinnamon would've been way too much for you."

Jem took another long sip. It was really good this way. Some of that joy he'd felt this morning filtered back with the thoughtfulness Murphy had just demonstrated. He *knew* him. Better than nearly anybody else.

They would be okay. They had to be okay, because this time, Jem knew what he'd be losing, and he'd fight for them with every ounce of himself.

He hadn't loved Murphy like this before.

But now that he did, he sure as hell wasn't going to let him go. Even if he had to be patient and prove himself. He could do that. He'd do much harder things, just to preserve this magic between them.

"It's perfect," Jem said and basked in the warmth of Murphy's smile.

Frosting squirted out the back of Murphy's piping bag, awkward in his big hand, and he swore as the sweet soupy mess coated his hand. "Goddamn it," he muttered.

"You okay?" Jem asked as he sprinkled one of his cookies with red and green jimmies.

"You'd just think a cookie exchange would be more *eating* and less *decorating*."

"Hey, at least you're artistic," Jem retorted.

Murphy didn't know if he was artistic in *this* way. Give him a piece of wood and he could absolutely carve something amazing. But flat cookies and this wet, goopy frosting? A freaking disaster.

"Maybe I'll just dip this whole thing in those sprinkles," Murphy said. "Sprinkles cover a multitude of sins."

"That sounds like a plan."

"You think anyone's gonna even want these?" Murphy said a few minutes later. The sprinkle dipping method was going well, so well, he'd implemented a *frosting* dipping method too, just dunking them right into the bowl of gloop and then into the sprinkles. Maybe the cookies wouldn't be edible, but nobody said they *had* to be.

Cookies could be delicious or they could be attractive. It seemed impossible to achieve both.

"I wouldn't even be surprised if we had a line," Jem said wryly.

"That's 'cause you're famous." People would probably sell these on eBay, like that grilled cheese with Jesus miraculously imprinted in the crust.

"And you're an artist." Jem grinned, waggling his eyebrows. "We're a dynamite combination."

Murphy turned back to his cookies. He knew what Jem was trying to say.

What he'd been trying to say for days, now.

Why was he so fucking afraid of just leaning over and kissing Jem, right here, where everyone could see? It wasn't like they hadn't seen his truck at Jem's cottage or Jem's car at his own place, more than once.

But every time he thought about the whole town knowing *for sure* that he and Jem were no longer just friends, he mentally freaked out.

Surely the only way to preserve this amazing turn of events was to keep it under wraps. If everyone knew, if they started gossiping about him and Jem even more than they already were, maybe Jem would start listening.

Maybe he'd realize that this was crazy. That he didn't really want to stay here in Christmas Falls, and that he didn't really want Murphy after all. That he wasn't worth all this bother and fuss.

When it was just the two of them, curled up in Jem's bed at the Snowman Cottages, or laughing in the shower at his place, it was easier to breathe. Easier to just relax into how perfect the two of them were together. He'd imagined what being with Jem might be like, way more times than he felt comfortable admitting to, and yet it was so much more unbelievably amazing than he'd ever dreamt it could be.

Now that he knew that, too, how could he ever give it up? Give Jem up?

He couldn't.

Not yet.

"Oh, good, you two are here," Griff said, stopping in front of their table, looking so much lighter than Jem remembered. Because Griff hadn't ever struck him as a particularly cheerful person, but he seemed a bit...happier...the last few times they'd seen each other.

"Here we are," Jem said lightly.

Murphy could tell he looked worried but was trying to pretend otherwise.

"If only you'd been on time *yesterday*, and the other night at the wine tasting," Griff said in a gruff voice.

They'd made sure to be on time today, even Jem keeping his hands to himself as he'd showered after his workout. But Murphy wondered if Jem was more worried about Griff's reaction than he'd let on.

Because he could feel Jem tensing next to him at Griff's gentle admonition.

"Yeah, I'm real sorry about that," Jem said in a serious voice.

"Hmmm," Griff said. He turned to Murphy. "I thought you were supposed to be keeping him in line, not letting him off the hook or leading him astray."

"I'm not," Murphy stuttered. The knowing look in Griff's eyes made it clear he knew the truth about what was really going on between them. That Murphy wasn't just Jem's liaison anymore.

"Murphy's been great," Jem said firmly.

"Just try to keep your hands to yourselves at the family events, okay?" Griff said in a kind but firm voice.

"We don't...we aren't..." Murphy stumbled, but before he could get the lie out, Griff was gone.

Jem turned to him. "Well, that could've been worse," he said. Actually sounding *relieved*.

But Murphy didn't feel better. He felt like fucking garbage. Like he'd been doing exactly what Griff had insinuated: distracting Jem by leading him around by his dick.

"I don't see how," Murphy said despondently. This was why he didn't want people to know. They'd wonder what the fuck the great Jem Knight was doing with *him*.

Even though Griff hadn't said it, and Griff and he were friends, and Griff even *liked* him, Murphy had felt the weight of his gaze. The judgment in it.

"You realize Griff was annoyed with *me,* right?" Jem asked. "I was the one who made us late."

"Yeah, 'cause of me," Murphy said.

"I couldn't say, *yet,* just how fucking irresistible you are, and that was the whole problem," Jem teased. "Lighten up, it's fine.

It's all fine. Come on, you can't sulk with a cookie in your mouth."

"I don't have—" But Murphy didn't get the rest of his sentence out because Jem was shoving a whole cookie, peanut butter chocolate chip, from the looks of it, and the *taste*, into his mouth.

"See?" Jem laughed. "You can't."

Murphy chewed the cookie and swallowed, glancing surreptitiously over to Jem, who was grinning with delight, like he'd just won the war.

But he'd just taken the first battle.

"Oh?" Murphy said and reached up with one of his still-wet cookies, coated with icing and sprinkles, and smeared it all over Jem's face.

He burst into laughter and then had to evade another glob of frosting Jem lobbed in his direction.

"Children!" Marlene called out. "Behave yourselves!"

But Griff had disappeared, and Murphy wasn't going to let Jem take him, even if he *was* an NFL player. Or had been, anyway.

He dodged him, running around the tables, and they ended up outside a minute later, Jem tackling him to the ground, the remainder of snow cushioning their fall.

Jem was laughing and Murphy couldn't help but join in, chuckling right along with him.

Leaning in, Murphy swiped his tongue up Jem's cheek, the frosting melting on his tongue.

"You're so sweet," Murphy murmured, still giggling under his breath as they sat up.

"I think that's not me," Jem retorted, but he was smiling, too.

Marlene appeared at the doorway, hands on her hips. "It's like you two are still ten years old," she said, but there was an undeniable glimmer of amusement in her gaze as she stared at them. "At least, you decided to take it outside before you destroyed the cookie exchange."

"Didn't want to let Griff down again," Jem said seriously.

Murphy elbowed him when she turned back around to go inside. "Still the suck-up, I see, trying to pretend like you didn't start it."

"What, me?" Jem asked innocently as they got up, leaning on each other.

"Yep, butter wouldn't melt in your mouth," Murphy teased.

"Or frosting."

"That too."

"Guess we'd better go back in. Don't want Marlene to kill us," Murphy said. He felt reluctant. Out here, nobody was around and he could stay like this, leaning on Jem. Absorbing the glorious warmth and weight of his body.

Jem caught his arm before he could turn to go inside. "Hey," he said, his gray eyes suddenly very serious. "I don't know what's up with you, but we can't keep doing this. I want to tell people we're together."

Murphy didn't want to panic, but he kinda did. "Oh?"

"You know I want to," Jem said, frowning. "It's time. This is a thing now, a real thing. A *relationship*. We can't just keep pretending we're two young kids, fucking around, like Marlene said."

"We didn't fuck around when we were ten," Murphy said, trying to change the subject, but Jem was like a dog with a bone. It was what had made him such an incredible football player—and an incredible lover too, for that matter. And also incredibly, horribly annoying as a person.

"You know what I mean," Jem said.

He did. And yet whenever he thought about it, of taking Jem's hand and walking inside and letting everyone say what they wanted, he felt hot and also cold, all over.

"I'll..." Murphy hesitated. Hating the look of resignation and frustration on Jem's face. Hating that he'd put it there. He only ever wanted to see the smile. "I'll think about it, okay? We'll get there."

Jem shot him a look. "Soon, okay? I hate this feeling that I'm like, screwing around with you. I don't want anyone to think that."

"I don't think they do," Murphy said optimistically, but the truth was probably a lot closer to what Jem had just said.

But what if they knew it was serious?

It wouldn't be a fun, frothy gossip story anymore. They'd get concerned. They'd get worried.

For Jem and about Jem and frankly, probably for Murphy, too.

In the end, nothing good would come from it.

"I care about you, a lot," Jem said softly and reached out, squeezed his hand, and then, because he was also one of the best people Murphy had ever known, let go again.

Wasn't going to push Murphy to do something he didn't want to do, even if he hated it.

And somehow, that made this whole thing even worse. Because there was no question in Murphy's mind that Jem Knight was the man for him.

Always had been.

And always would be.

Chapter 13

Jem didn't realize how much he'd begun to count on Murphy's presence at these festival events until this afternoon, when Murph had sent him a text claiming he had some work he needed to catch up on.

Jem couldn't exactly be mad about it. After all, they'd been spending a ton of time together, so much that Jem had been surprised, because surely Murph had to work? But he kept claiming this was actually the slow part of his season. So he hadn't been surprised to get his text.

Disappointed, but not surprised.

Still, he hadn't expected how much he'd come to rely on him to be a buffer until he wasn't here tonight.

Also, Jem could make small talk, but something called a *social*, apparently just meant that everyone milled around, drinking hot chocolate, piling cookies and marshmallows and sprinkles on top of the mountains of whipped cream in their mug.

The sugar was the only advantage of this, Jem thought morosely, trying not to sulk about the fact that he was currently hiding by this far wall, hoping that nobody else would notice him and come up to ask about what the Condors were currently going through.

He didn't know what to say about it, only that Deacon insisted, every time he asked, that they were handling it and Jem didn't need to come back to Charleston.

Jem had tried asking more than once exactly how Deacon was handling it, because there was definitely a story there—and with Mr. G, the Condors' owner, no less—but Deacon had developed an annoying habit of not responding whenever he asked about it.

The end result was that he knew nothing, and no amount of pumping him for information was going to give the curious the details, or the gossip, that they were looking for.

There was only so much Jem could smile and nod and take another long drink of cocoa, to avoid saying anything.

He was still hiding when Tasha approached, her magenta hair bright in the room. Her hands were cradled around her mug, nails painted neon orange.

Jem eyed her drink. "Do you have any cocoa under all that whipped cream?"

"Cocoa *and* Bailey's," Tasha said smugly.

"Ugh," Jem said. "Don't tell me you smuggled that in?"

"Clearly you're an amateur, still. The only way to come to these is to fortify yourself with at least one shot in your mug." She paused, glancing around. "Is Murphy not here with you?"

"He said he had some work to catch up on," Jem said. Surely Tasha would have known about it, if Murphy had to work?

Or what if he'd just bailed on the cocoa social because he hadn't wanted Jem to push him again about going public?

Ugh, he didn't really regret making his feelings known, and he was *willing* to be patient, if that was what Murphy needed, but it seemed there might be more going on than just Murphy's fear of gossip. Because everyone was already talking about them. Going public would at least cut down on the rampant speculation on what was going on by making crystal clear exactly what was going on.

"Oh, so he's avoiding you," Tasha said.

Jem made a face. "He is?"

She waved a hand. "It's really not all that surprising, when you think about it."

"It's not?" It was surprising—and more than a little disap-pointing—to Jem. "I don't want him to avoid me. I..." Jem stopped short of telling Tasha that he loved him.

The first person he was going to say that to was Murphy himself.

If the man would *let* him.

"I know," Tasha said, like she actually did know. "He's being very, very stupid."

Jem took a long drink of cocoa, wishing that unlike his own G-rated cocoa, he had some of Tasha's Bailey's in there. "Any advice on how to get him to be *not* stupid?"

"I'm sure you're already being patient," Tasha said. "If you weren't, you wouldn't be tolerating all these idiots pumping you for details about the Condors."

"Yeah, well," Jem said, chuckling weakly. "I was hiding, 'cause I was sorta done tolerating that. But yeah, I'm trying to be pa-tient with him. I know it's a lot to expect, to adjust his thinking to how we are now."

Tasha shot him a look over the rim of her mug. "Yeah, uh-huh, definitely a big adjustment." Her wry voice made it clear there was something she—and *Murphy*—were not telling him.

"Any other advice?"

"Keep being patient."

"That's—"

But Tasha interrupted him, putting a hand on his arm. "Just trust me on this one. He's not panicking because he's gotten into this and he doesn't know how to get out. He never wants to get out. Not when it's you."

"Ah, okay." Jem wasn't sure he was quite the catch Tasha made him sound like, but since this was Murphy, he wouldn't argue about it. He'd just take it. After all, he *wanted* the guy to like him. To love him, even, the way Jem loved him back.

Jem cleared his throat. "So when he avoids me," he continued, "should I..."

"That time is rapidly coming to a close, I promise." Tasha sounded very sure of this. Jem wasn't sure how she could be *so* certain, but it was undeniable.

"If you're sure..."

"I'm sure." Tasha patted him on the arm and drained the rest of her cocoa in one long gulp. "I gotta run, but good talk. Just remember what I said, okay?"

He watched her go, realizing as she blew out of Jolly Java that she hadn't really said *anything*. Not anything specific, anyway.

What was he supposed to do? Be patient? Well, he could do that. It wasn't easy, not when he wanted so goddamn much, but he could do anything at all.

Anything except lose Murphy.

"You are a total idiot."

Murphy glanced up from the carving he was working on to see Tasha standing there, shutting the door to his workshop behind her.

"I thought you were going to the cocoa social," Murphy said absently as he leaned in and chiseled a little bit of wood and then sat back again. Trying to decide if he should take more off.

He'd wanted to go with her, because Jem had invited him.

But for the last few days, he'd been wrestling with the fact that Jem had asked him to think about going public, about deciding he didn't give a crap what the rest of the town thought, and the problem with that request was that Murphy hadn't thought about *anything else*. And he still wasn't any closer to feeling like he was ready to take the risk.

You can't lose him. Not now, not when you know what it's like to have him.

When Tasha didn't respond, just stared at him with her arms crossed in front of her chest, he added, "You even filled up your little silver flask with Bailey's. You never go to the cocoa social without fortification."

"I was there," she said. "Jem was there, too."

"Yeah," Murphy responded, trying for casual and ending up somewhere near defensive. "He said he was going."

"And *you* were supposed to go, too," Tasha said. "He said you bailed on him. To *work*."

"This is an important piece," Murphy defended. Some days it felt like the most important gnome he'd ever carve, though that could hardly be true.

But it still felt like it, deep down, in a very black-and-white place Murphy didn't know how to argue with.

Tasha walked over, standing next to him as he examined the hair of the gnome again. It didn't quite feel right. There was something a little off about it, and he'd been working on it for hours now, trying to get it just right.

Trying to make it perfect.

"It's a beautiful piece," Tasha said softly.

Murphy swallowed hard. Took out his smallest chisel and cut one of the grooves a little deeper. Initially he'd wanted to hide it from Tasha, but she was his best friend and his business partner, and the workshop was her workspace, too. He couldn't hide it for long.

The first time she'd seen it, she'd cried. The second time, she'd just given him a pointed look, her gaze shifting between the carving and his face.

But now it seemed she was ready to talk about it.

"You love him," she said.

Murphy didn't know what to say to that. He felt like it was obvious. Like it had *always* been obvious.

"You've always loved him," she added. Making it clear she could read him the same as she always had.

"Yes," Murphy said.

"He doesn't know."

"That I loved him then or that I love him now?"

"Either one," Tasha said.

"If you say I should just tell him, I...that's crazy, Tash."

"Don't say that you can't, because you can. The guy's wild for you. He wants everyone to know that you're his and he's *yours*. Why are you fighting this? Why haven't you told him the truth about high school?"

"How do you know I haven't?" It was purely a stalling tactic. Murphy knew it. Tasha knew it. But he did it anyway.

"Because Jem said to me tonight maybe you needed time to *adjust to seeing him in a new light*." Tasha gave him a look. "You've never needed to adjust. What you needed to do was tell him the fucking truth. Back then. And even more so, *now*. Especially because now he feels the same way you do."

"You don't know that either," Murphy retorted.

"I see the way he looks at you. I know how patient he's being when you're being an idiot. Someone who loved you less wouldn't be willing to wait around while you figure your shit out, Murph."

"I don't have anything to figure out." Except that he knew he did. It was so annoying how well Tasha knew him.

"Murphy." She took him by the arm and turned him to face her. She put her hands on his shoulders. "You love him. He loves you. You've just got to be honest and get out of your own way."

"I wish it was that easy."

"Except that *yeah*, it is," Tasha said firmly. "You sit him down and say, I didn't feel like I could tell you the truth about high school, but now, with this new relationship, I need to come clean. You tell him everything: exactly how you feel, that you love him. That you've always loved him. That you want to be with him."

"But what if he...what if we..." Murphy stuttered and looked away. He didn't want Tasha to see the fear in his eyes.

Because he was fucking afraid.

"This season's been magical for you, Murph," she said gently. "For both of you."

"And what if the magic ends?"

"Then real life begins, and it's not easy, for sure, but I think with how long you've been pining after this guy, you'd want to fight for a life with him. Fight for *him*. Cause I believe with every bone in my body that he'd fight for you."

"You think?" It was terrifying to think she might be wrong. Even more terrifying that she might be right.

"Yes," Tasha said firmly. "The man loves you. He's yours if you want him. And I think you do."

Murphy took a deep breath. Stared at the carving in front of him. He hadn't had to go this particular direction with this. He could have just carved a gnome with the ideas Jem had given him originally. But he'd looked at the wood block he'd lugged in here and seen something so different, the kind of future he'd always been too afraid to dream of.

"I felt like if I could do this, if I could *see* it come to life with my hands, maybe I'd have the courage to make it true."

"Murph," Tasha said gently, wrapping her arms around his waist and hugging him tight, "it's *already* true. You just have to accept it."

Murphy thought of how wonderful the last few weeks had been. That first night, Jem's interested gaze on his face, his body. The way he'd wanted to make sure Murphy was comfortable with what Griff had asked of him. The wonder on his face when he'd seen the Santa gnome Murphy had carved in Sugar Plum Park. The tender eagerness in his kiss. The incandescent heat between them. The way Jem's eyes still crinkled when he smiled, same as they had twenty-five years ago, twenty years ago, fifteen years ago, and now.

The patience that he'd exhibited.

The kindness and generosity every time someone asked him for an autograph or a selfie.

Jeremiah Knight had always been larger than life, and he still was, it was undeniable, but somehow, Murphy realized that he'd grown, too, until the only thing keeping them apart was his own inability to see clearly.

He cleared his throat and turned to his best friend. "Thank you, Tasha," he said resolutely.

She smiled. "Go get your man, Murph."

Jem was standing in front of the open fridge, absently scratching at his chest, wishing he'd thought to throw a T-shirt on, along with his gray sweatpants, when he'd come home from the social.

He was debating between leftover meatloaf from the White Elephant and constructing himself a big turkey club sandwich when there was a knock on his door.

Jem thought it might be Felix, come to ask more advice about his boss, maybe, or to give Jem the new scoop on what was going on between them. He certainly was curious to see how that had turned out but he'd been so busy with Murphy recently he hadn't had a chance to ask Felix about it.

But when he pulled the door open, it wasn't Felix standing there, but Murphy. Looking uneasy but resolved.

Tasha had told him to hold tight, and he'd wondered if she'd talk to Murphy.

Well, whatever she'd said—or whatever he'd decided—Murphy was here now.

"Hey," Jem said, waving him inside. It was cold as hell and he rubbed his chest again. Wished again he'd put a shirt on. But then Murphy wouldn't be looking at him like that if he had. "Thought you were working tonight. I was gonna make a sandwich. You want one?"

Murphy looked confused. "Want what?"

"A sandwich," Jem said.

"Oh, yeah. Uh. Sure." Murphy trailed after Jem as they walked into the tiny kitchen.

Jem opened the fridge door and began to pull out sliced meat and cheese, pickles, mayo, and the special horseradish mustard he liked that he thought Murphy would also enjoy.

"I was working," Murphy said before Jem could turn around. "I really was. I just...I was avoiding you, too."

"I know," Jem said softly. He shut the fridge door and glanced behind him before he grabbed the bread from the counter.

"You do?"

"Murph—you're not that hard for me to read. We've known each other a long time. You're still Murphy. You haven't changed much."

"You haven't changed at all," Murphy said wryly. "You're still...you're still so fucking bright, Jem."

Jem smiled. "Yeah?"

"I should have told you this before," Murphy said in a rush. "Should have told you this when you came back to town. Should have probably told you this way back when, before you ever *left* town. I...I was so crazy about you, back then. That's why we stopped being friends. I had...probably the world's biggest, and most hopeless, crush on you."

Jem dropped the butter knife he was holding. "You *what*?"

When he glanced over at Murphy, he had a sheepish look on his face. "Yeah," he said.

"You—"

"Was absolutely head-over-heels crazy about you in a way I knew you'd never return? Yeah."

Jem could barely believe it. But then he could, too. With that new information, the secret Murphy had been hiding all this time, so many things made more sense.

"You didn't want to tell me back then," Jem said slowly. He put his hands onto Murphy's shoulders, and he could tell Murphy wanted to look away but he didn't. He faced Jem's gaze head-on.

"Of course not," Murphy retorted. "I told you it was *hopeless*. You were Jem Knight, and I was—"

"You were Murphy Clark," Jem said firmly. "You were my best friend. I loved you. As a friend, yeah. Maybe I would've loved you as more, if you'd just *said*."

"It wasn't that easy back then. Things were different, you were leaving town, and I knew that, and I thought, maybe easier to just...make the break clean."

It made a strange kind of sense.

It pissed Jem off, too.

But he could see why Murphy had done it.

Especially if he'd thought it was hopeless.

"Did you ever regret it?" Jem asked quietly. Because he'd regretted how their friendship had ended, lots of times. He could look back, clear-eyed, and see that now. That maybe he'd thrown himself into all those sports and all those activities and even all those dreams because he'd been hurting so much over losing the person he'd loved above all others.

"All the time," Murphy said.

"Then I came back to town, and I hit on you..."

"I still wanted you. I didn't think I could have you, but then you did that." Murphy shrugged.

Jem framed his face with his hands. His beloved face. "You've always had me," he said seriously. "Back then, and now, and forever. I love you, Murphy Clark."

"Like a friend or..." Murphy trailed off awkwardly, and Jem could only chuckle.

"Like a friend and a lover and everything else in-between. I could never figure out why I never wanted anyone permanent. Because the only person I've ever wanted was *you*."

Murphy squeezed his eyes shut. "I can't believe it." When he opened them, they were glowing warm, the love in them unmistakable.

Jem had hoped his feelings were returned, but this was more than he'd ever imagined.

"I love you, Murphy," he repeated. Leaned in to kiss him.

But before he could, Murphy murmured back, "Jeremiah Knight, I love you too."

They'd shared so many kisses over the last few magical weeks, but this kiss, in the dim kitchen with Jem halfway through making sandwiches and wearing only a pair of old, ratty sweatpants, Murphy's plaid coat cold against his skin, left all of them in the dust.

It was the best gift Jem could ever think of.

Maybe because it was a gift they shared.

CHAPTER 14

"DID YOU REALLY THINK telling everyone would mean they'd convince me to leave you?" Jem asked in a teasing voice.

Murphy shot him a look but there was no denying it was a lot warmer and sweeter than it had ever been before. He was crazy in love with Jem, and miraculously, Jem seemed to be just as in love with him.

He still couldn't quite believe it, even though Jem kept saying it, like he knew Murphy had this voice in the back of his head that still occasionally whispered that he was imagining this whole thing and it wasn't real and Jem didn't love him after all.

But he did.

Murphy *knew* he did, and as Christmas grew closer, one day melting into the next, Murphy existing in a haze of loved-up euphoria, that voice began to die out.

And now tonight, at the Ugly Christmas Sweater Party, one of Christmas Falls' most important events, he'd managed to quiet it enough that he'd agreed to coming not as longtime friends, but as a couple.

"You know that was something I worried about," Murphy said.

Jem wrapped an arm around his shoulders, tugging him close. "Yeah, and it's a little ridiculous, Murph. Remember my parents? They thought I'd break *your* heart."

"Maybe we should've done way less listening to them and more listening to ourselves," Murphy said.

"Always," Jem said.

More people had begun to filter into the White Elephant from the ice sculpture contest final. He and Jem hadn't missed that either, but he'd insisted on leaving right after the announcement of the winner—which Murphy had been thrilled to hear was Carl—so they could get a prime spot at the White Elephant.

Not a booth, he'd said to Jem as they'd entered the restaurant, *I want a table in the middle of the whole freaking room.*

Jem's answering smile had been worth how scary it had been to say.

"I can't believe you got me in this sweater," Jem groused as the waitress approached with their drinks. Beer for his guy, and because Murphy had decided to say *screw it* to everything, he'd gotten a sugar cookie martini.

"It's cute on you," Murphy pointed out, though frankly *everything* was cute on Jem. Especially nothing at all.

But really, Jem telling him he loved him wearing just a pair of old gray sweatpants had been the pinnacle of his entire life. There was no way Murphy was ever getting over that. Or the way his ass had been outlined in the worn material when he'd turned around...

Not now, Murphy reminded his brain (and his cock). *You're at a semi family friendly event, and you don't need to slobber all over your boyfriend.*

Except that was all he really wanted to do.

As far as he was concerned, they could do some big public kiss under the prominently hanging bundle of mistletoe in the center of the room and then bail.

The mistletoe was only a few feet away. He'd just need to get Jem up and maneuver him over there...

"Are you even listening to me?" Jem asked with amusement. "You're staring at that mistletoe. Do you really want to lean into that particular cliche?"

"Is it really a cliche if it works?" Murphy questioned. But the truth was, no, he didn't want to kiss and run either. Jem deserved more than that, and he'd wanted this. Impossibly, unbelievably, he wanted everyone to know Murphy belonged to him. Like being with Murphy was so awesome he could barely wait to brag about it.

And you're gonna enjoy it. Every goddamn second of it.

That voice didn't even belong to Tasha; it was one hundred percent Murphy Clark.

"Noted," Jem said, grinning. He leaned in, brushing a light kiss onto Murphy's bearded cheek.

"Jeremiah Knight, and who is this you're kissing? Oh, Murphy, of course it's you." Mrs. Lil smiled as she stared down at them, at their tangled fingers sitting prominently on the table. "After that exhibition at the pie bakeoff, I can't say any of us are really so surprised. Though you, young man," she added, glancing pointedly over at Jem, "are going to have to be around a lot more now."

"That's the plan, Mrs. Lil," Jem said firmly. "Couldn't be without my man here. Not when he makes me so happy."

Her face softened even further. "Some of us," she said, "knew this was happening from the moment you two stole that pie from your granny, Murphy. I'm so glad you two finally saw it, too."

"What?" Murphy squawked. He'd finally made his peace with Christmas Falls knowing, but what if they knew about his *long-term* crush? That would be—

Awesome. Absolutely freaking awesome. That voice did belong to Tasha.

Mrs. Lil raised an eyebrow.

"I should've seen it sooner," Jem said regretfully. He glanced over at Murphy and squeezed his hand. "Sorry, Murph."

"No," Murphy said, shaking his head and suddenly feeling very sure he was right. "No, it was right. You went off and conquered your dreams. I found my own. If we'd been…if we'd been involved back then, it wouldn't have happened like that. Maybe it wouldn't have even lasted…"

Jem's hand tightened in his. "Yeah?"

"Yeah," Murphy said with every ounce of certainty he could. "It was right, this time around. Down to you not recognizing me in Frosty's that very first night."

"You did not," Mrs. Lil said with a shocked gasp.

"I did not," Jem confirmed wryly.

"Oh, that is just so cute. And you probably flirted with him, having *no idea* he was your best friend when you two were kids. That's such a perfect story. We should get Emerson to write it."

"Emerson?"

"Oh," Mrs. Lil said earnestly, "he's this very nice young man. Staying over at Arlo's. He's a writer! Imagine that. A writer in our little town. Not like Frank. Emerson always has a nice dose of romance in his books," She paused. "Not that you're not *very* impressive, Jeremiah."

"Thanks," Jem said dryly.

"Just a little *less* impressive than Emerson," Mrs. Lil said.

Murphy laughed. "I don't know, Mrs. Lil, I find Jem pretty dang impressive."

"Well, of course, dear. You're supposed to. Now, I'm going to go get one of those hot toddies. But before I go—your sweater is really darling, Jeremiah. I'm definitely going to vote for you."

Jem groaned as she walked away. "I should've told her that this was *your* sweater, that you were planning on making this *balls to the walls* statement." He shifted around, jingling the bells strung across his chest on purpose, and Murphy couldn't help but laugh.

"But would I have ever worn it in public? That's the question."

Jem shot him a look. "I'm unsure why your current attire isn't just as groundbreaking."

Murphy knew how red he was flushing. "Well, I wasn't planning on wearing this one either."

Jem gave him an appraising look, then his gaze drifted lower, to where the reindeer were mounting each other in a line across his chest. "I don't know," he said, "I think it's kinda cute. Maybe we should re-enact it later."

"Maybe," Murphy said, flushing even redder.

"Hey, you're the one who wanted to do this today," Jem said. "And we didn't have to wear an ugly Christmas sweater, either.

We could have come dressed perfectly normally, had a drink, kissed under that mistletoe, and then called it good."

"I wanted to do it right. Do right by you," Murphy said.

Jem's expression softened from amusement to pure, unadulterated love. "And that," he murmured, "is exactly why I love you."

Murphy cleared his throat. "You wanna go...uh...do that mistletoe thing now?"

"Aw, so eager to claim me, huh?" Jem teased.

If he had any idea.

Oh wait. He did now, because Murphy had finally confessed the truth. The funny thing about secrets was even when they were out in the open, it was hard to adjust to the new truth. He still wasn't used to it.

"Yeah," Murphy said. He took a long sip of his drink. The sweet sugary taste hit his tongue, and the alcohol hit a moment later, warming him up everywhere. It was easier then to say, "Always wanted to do it."

"God, come 'ere," Jem said roughly and then he was tugging him into a warm, insistent kiss. It was so easy to sink into it, to let the rest of the White Elephant fall away and all the people who were almost certainly watching them until all he could feel and taste and smell was Jem.

It was almost certainly less PG-rated—and with a lot more tongue—than Griff probably would've liked while they were officially representing the festival, but then, Murphy had seen Griff and his guy around town recently, and it wasn't like they were pretending they weren't crazy about each other either.

When they broke apart, Murphy realized that he didn't feel afraid at all. Not that Jem would freak out, or that someone would say something and make him realize that he was wrong about Murphy after all. Because there was no way you could move Jem if he believed in something.

And the way he was looking at Murphy now, he was all the way in, believing in Murphy to the core of his being.

"Did you mean that?" Jem asked in a hushed voice.

"The kiss?" Murphy knew how lust-stupid he sounded, but it wasn't entirely his fault; he wasn't sure how much blood was really left in his brain. After they finished their drinks and could *finally* leave, he was going to need a moment to make sure his arousal wasn't painfully obvious in his jeans. His plaid coat would only cover so many sins—and nobody had ever gotten him worked up the way Jem did.

Jem shook his head. "What you said earlier. To Mrs. Lil about us being right for each other *now*, but not back then. In high school."

The part of Murphy that was still that high school kid, painfully awkward and crushing so hopelessly on the most popular guy in school—a guy Murphy *knew* was the best guy in the world, too, because Jem had been by his side for nearly their whole lives—shrieked inside, but Murphy turned his back on that kid.

He wasn't that kid any longer.

"Yeah, I meant it," Murphy said.

They'd have made a complete fucking mess of it, if they'd tried to be together then. Murphy hadn't known what he wanted in life. He'd only wanted Jem, and if he'd gotten him, he knew the relationship wouldn't have been balanced or healthy. And God knew, Jem wanted to make him happy—he'd wanted to do it, even then—and maybe back then, Murphy would've been selfish and desperate enough to let him stay, even though it wasn't his dream.

They'd have ended up breaking up, disillusioned, like so many young couples did after high school.

Maybe he'd have had Jem for a few years, but now, Murphy really hoped that he might have Jem *forever*.

"I've tried to tell myself that I wasn't stupid, not seeing what was right in front of my face," Jem said quietly. "But maybe I wasn't stupid."

"I do wish I'd done one thing differently," Murphy said, finishing his martini.

Jem drained the rest of his beer, and they stood, Jem's palm warm and reassuring against his lower back.

"What's that?" Jem asked.

"I wish I hadn't shut you out. I wish we'd stayed friends, this whole time."

He felt Jem's fingers tighten against his back, even through his coat.

"Yeah?" Jem said.

"I was a coward," Murphy said, "and I'm sorry."

"You said that, before."

"I'm not sure I did, not in as many words, and I should've." Murphy took a deep breath of the cold air as they exited the White Elephant and its noise and light. They'd walked from Jem's cottage to Santa's Village, and it would be a cold, brisk walk home. But he had the man he loved to keep him warm.

"Ah, uh, well, maybe you didn't." Jem shrugged awkwardly.

"I mean it," Murphy said. It felt natural to reach out and tangle their hands together as they turned the corner around the White Elephant. He'd been so afraid of this for so long, but all that fear was gone, once and for all.

"I know you do. And you know what? I shouldn't have you let you do it, but I did. We both screwed this up, but it's not screwed up anymore. Now, it's perfect." Jem grinned at him. "Come on, let's go home."

"Hey, look, that wasn't there earlier," Murphy said, gesturing to the back side of the White Elephant, a two-story wall that reached up towards the sky. It was normally plain brick, but tonight, it was painted with gnomes. At least a dozen of them.

Big ones and short ones. Gnomes of all shapes and sizes, holding hands and lifting their faces to the painted sky, where, in a big banner of red and green, was emblazoned, *family*.

"That must be one of those graffiti paintings Griff was complaining about before," Jem said.

"I know he was all worked up about it, thought it was 'destructive' or something, but I think it's pretty cool. Those gnomes, you know they're not all related. But they're still family." Murphy knew that family wasn't just the people you were related to, but everyone who cared about you, that you cared about in return. And he was undeniably pleased to have the artist make the same point he'd been espousing for years now.

"Yeah, they're still family. And more," Jem said steadily, looking straight at Murphy. Love in his eyes.

Jem backed up against the wall and turned, holding his phone up. "Come 'ere," he said. "Let's take a picture. Our first graffiti selfie."

"First selfie, period," Murphy teased, but he was clearly delighted, still.

They took the picture, Jem juggling his phone and then Murphy juggling his, trying to get the best angle before they both dissolved into laughter.

"You posting that?" Murphy asked as they finally got back on the sidewalk, headed to Jem's cottage. But Jem's attention was focused on his phone.

"Yeah, and I'm gonna send it to my guys, too," Jem said. He glanced over at Murphy. "That okay? I just thought it was a super-cool idea, and I love how we look in front of it. Don't you?"

Murphy nodded. "Tag me, okay?"

Jem raised an eyebrow.

"I'm serious," Murphy said. "I don't mind if everyone knows. Everyone who already matters *knows* anyway. They all saw tonight."

"And they probably knew anyway?" Jem asked archly.

Murphy laughed in agreement. "Yeah, probably," he admitted.

Jem finished with his phone and tucked it into his pocket. "There, all done," he said, sounding very satisfied with himself.

"You said you sent it to 'your guys' too?" Murphy asked.

"Yeah, my teammates that I'm close to. They're my family, too, but then, you probably already knew that," Jem said.

"Yeah, I did." It was clear from the way Jem talked about Deacon and the rest of the Condors how much they meant to him. How much it had sucked to not be playing with them for the rest of the season.

Jem's phone started vibrating in his pocket. "Oh, God," he said, pulling it out, a wide grin on his face.

"What is it?"

"Oh, they're just…" Jem laughed. "Giving me a ton of shit. But they're happy for me too. They think you're a very sexy lumberjack."

"What do you think?" Murphy asked, making a little bit of a joke out of it because not once, in any of his thirty-three years, had he felt he was very sexy. Except maybe when he was naked and Jem was about to pounce.

"I think…" Jem hesitated and Murphy elbowed him hard in the stomach and they both nearly went down laughing. "I think you're a very, *very* sexy lumberjack."

"God, you're so gorgeous like this," Murphy murmured into the silence stretching out between them.

Jem arched his back and groaned a little. Trying to entice Murphy to stop *looking* and start *doing*.

"When I said I wanted to re-enact your sweater," Jem said, straining for his lover's touch, "I kinda thought you were gonna move faster than the figures."

"Jem, those figures weren't *moving* at all," Murphy pointed out, so reasonably, so logically. So lucidly.

Jem did not feel lucid.

He felt like living fire, just barely contained by his skin. Everywhere Murph had touched him felt more alive than he ever had before.

His cock bobbed, hard as it had ever been, still wet from Murphy's mouth as he'd sucked him and begun to finger him open, slow as molasses, until Jem was just about crazy with wanting it.

"Yeah, I *know*," Jem said with another groan. "Come on, I'm ready, I swear."

"Not to brag, but I'm not exactly small."

But at least instead of continuing to clench around nothing, Jem nearly bit his tongue off as Murphy tucked his fingers back inside him.

Jem moaned loudly, losing himself in the feel of Murphy's big, calloused fingers thrusting inside him.

"Just wanna take care of you," Murphy muttered under his breath.

"Trust me, taking care of me is fucking me," Jem said, trying very hard not to wail as Murphy's fingers hit his prostate and massaged it insistently. "I'm gonna come all over this bed in a minute and that'll be a major disappointment."

"Nothing about you could ever be a disappointment," Murphy said with awe and love rich in his voice.

Jem decided he was not above begging. "Fuck me, *please*."

"So impatient," Murphy teased.

But he removed his fingers, and Jem could hear rustling behind him. God, he hoped Murphy was finally putting on a condom, because if he wasn't...

Jem only had a moment to prepare himself as Murphy's fingers suddenly dug insistently into his hips and he pulled him back, his cock snubbing up against his hole.

The slide was long and overwhelming, and Jem was pretty sure he was crying by the end of it. He *was* babbling incoherently, the length of Murphy's cock stealing what was left of his sanity.

He was only lust, and he wanted to come so badly he was nearly delirious with it.

"Is that okay?" Murphy was finally panting hard, too—Jem *did* register that, and there was a part of him that he'd acknowledge later that was very proud he'd unwound him even that much. "Are you okay?"

"I'm—" Jem bit off a groan as Murphy slid the rest of the way. "I'm so fucking good, if you don't—"

"I got you, baby," Murphy said reverently.

For a moment, Jem worried that maybe the reverence would mean it would be a slow, gentle kind of fuck.

But instead, Murphy grabbed him hard and proceeded to fuck him into the mattress. Perfectly. Flawlessly.

Until he *was* crying into the comforter, no question about it whatsoever.

"Come on, baby," Murphy crooned above him, his breath coming in shallow pants, "I wanna feel you come around me."

Jem knew he was close. It felt like he'd been right there on the edge the entire night, after he'd kissed Murphy right in the middle of the White Elephant and *definitely* once they'd come back to his cottage and they'd gotten naked, Murphy giving him so much goddamn foreplay he should've come half a dozen times before now.

"Harder," he panted and reached up, barely grazing his hard, leaking cock with his fingers, and that was all it took, his whole body bowed and he lost himself to the pleasure surging through him.

He heard Murphy behind him, felt his hips stutter, and his own cry.

Jem was curled up in the damp, disgusting blankets when Murphy came back from the bathroom a minute later.

"Hey, you good?" Murphy asked, bending over, a wet washcloth in one hand.

"Yes," Jem said, snatching it from his grip. Cleaned himself. He was capable of that, thank you very much. Of course, God only knew what he'd said, what he'd begged Murphy for. He'd never had anyone take him that far, and if he was being completely honest with himself, he'd loved every second of it.

A fact Murphy was very aware of, if the smug look on his face was any indication, as he crawled into bed next to Jem and pulled him close.

"You're so hot like that," Murphy said, sighing happily.

"I didn't say anything ridiculous?" Jem wasn't particularly worried, but he was curious. After all, Murphy already knew he loved him. What else could he say?

"You were perfect," Murphy insisted.

Jem raised an eyebrow.

"What?" Murphy questioned. "A gentleman doesn't kiss and tell."

"I was *there*, Murph," Jem teased.

"Oh trust me, I'm not gonna forget that anytime soon."

"No?" A feeling that had to be complete, incandescent happiness surged through Jem's chest. So that was what this really felt like. No wonder everyone went a little insane when they fell in love.

"Let's just say, thirteen-year-old Murphy would've been *very* happy," Murphy said. "And it turns out, so is thirty-three-year-old Murphy."

CHAPTER 15

"I'M SO GLAD THEY finally got all the snow up off the ground," Patricia Clark said, bustling into the living room with a huge platter shaped like a Christmas tree, nearly every inch filled with crackers, sliced meat, and sliced cheeses.

Murphy had learned better than to gorge himself on all the food his mother liked to put out *before* holiday meals, because if he did, he'd never be able to do the main event justice. But clearly Jem hadn't learned the way Murphy had, because he leaned in and picked up a rosette of salami, popping it in his mouth. And this was after he'd demolished half a tray of his mother's famous sweet and spicy mini franks.

He was going to be regretting all that intake in an hour, and Murphy considered warning him.

But it might also be more fun to see him groaning.

"Mom, there was barely any snow."

Patricia fixed him with a firm look. "Barely any snow? Then why did Jem's daddy have to spend all that time helping to clean it up?"

They'd spent last night, Christmas Eve, with Jem's parents, at the candlelight processional to Sugar Plum Park. Then the four of them had enjoyed a late-night dinner at the White Elephant before Murphy and Jem had returned to Jem's cottage for the night.

"I think he actually likes doing it," Jem volunteered, between bites of meat and cheese.

He was really going to regret that. Murphy elbowed him in the side and Jem shot him a questioning look.

"Too much food," Murphy hissed under his breath.

But Jem still looked confused, and his mother was off again. "Still, all those poor people trying to get home for Christmas. I'm just glad they could make it." She smiled warmly at Jem. "And speaking of being home for Christmas, I know you two don't like to talk about it—"

"It's not that we don't want to talk about it," Murphy interrupted. He'd worried Christmas was going to be this, his mother alternatively thrilled and curious about their relationship. "We're just...still figuring some stuff out."

But surprisingly, Christmas had been very easy. It had been unexpectedly simple to arrange Christmas Eve with Jem's parents and Christmas Day with Murphy's.

Like the arrangement had been waiting there on them, the whole time, and they just had to figure their own relationship out first.

"But," Patricia continued, undeterred by Murphy's interruption, "we're *very* happy to have you back home, and I'm sure Murphy is too."

"He's said as much," Jem said, an amused expression on his face as he glanced over at Murphy.

"Thrilled would be more like it," Murphy muttered.

"Are you staying around after the holidays? I'm sure you are." Patricia continued to chatter away. "You won't want to leave Murphy. You two have been so close recently. And I know Murphy—"

Murphy couldn't take it any longer. He turned to Jem, who was grinning. "Please kill me," he said. "I don't care that it's a holiday. Please just kill me and put me out of my misery."

"I don't know, you look like you're pretty happy," Jem teased.

"Murphy Anderson Clark," Patricia said firmly. "Jeremiah should know how much we like that he's around, for this town and for you."

"I do, Mrs. Clark, thank you," Jem said.

"And how happy we are that you two finally figured out you were more than friends," she said mischievously.

Murphy groaned again. "You wanna go see what my dad's doing?"

"I thought he was chopping wood?" Jem asked, clearly confused. "For the bonfire?"

One of the most important Clark Christmas traditions was the big bonfire at the end of the day. After they were all stuffed with roast beef, honey ham, mashed potatoes, his mother's famous braised brussels sprouts, and of course, the four different kinds of pie she always baked for the occasion, they'd gather around with cups of cider and hot chocolate, warm their bodies with the fire and watch the blanket of stars overhead.

Jem had come over for Christmas bonfires many times over the years.

In fact, before Murphy had killed their friendship at the beginning of high school, he'd never missed one.

"He is," Murphy confirmed.

"And he needs our help doing that?" Jem still looked confused. Murphy's dad was big and broad and even quieter than Murphy. He definitely did not need help chopping wood.

Jem probably wanted to continue sitting here, eating too many appetizers.

But Murphy was nervous and about to go out of his skin.

"Come on," he said, "I actually wanted to show you your gnome."

"Oh, you carved a gnome for Jem?" his mother exclaimed, looking thrilled. Probably planning their wedding in her head.

He dragged Jem outside, barely giving him enough time to get his coat on, before she could ask to come along.

Murphy hadn't been entirely convinced, not until Jem had told him he loved him, that he'd gone the right direction with the gnome.

After all, this wasn't exactly what Jem had asked for.

But why else had he carved it, if he wasn't going to give it to him?

It belonged to Jem. That much Murphy knew.

"I can see why you moved out," Jem teased as they walked through the woods that separated Murphy's parents' house from Murphy's own.

A few years back, he'd built his own little cabin and work-space on the other side of his parents' property.

"She means well," Murphy said. "She's just...excited. And happy for us."

"Well, I'm happy for us, too," Jem said, shoving his hands in his pockets, smiling as they crossed the little stream, over the bridge Murphy had built just after high school. "I didn't realize you'd already finished the gnome. Tasha told me she wasn't sure how it was coming along."

Tasha had told him a little white lie at Murphy's direction. Because he hadn't been sure he could show Jem what he'd carved.

But over the last week, he'd become so much more settled in Jem's love and affection. He knew he had it and there was no way it was going to disappear. Not now. He'd known then that he could not only give the gnome to Jem, but that there was no other gift he could give him for Christmas that would mean nearly as much.

They reached Murphy's workshop, and he unlocked the door, pushing it open.

"I know you told me what you were looking for," Murphy said, hesitating in the gloom, not wanting to flick the light on until he gave Jem some kind of explanation. "But when I started carving, the work took on a life of its own. Sometimes that happens."

Jem's gaze was steady on his. Full of love and support. *Unconditional* love and support.

"I know that whatever it is, Murph, I'm gonna love it," Jem said.

Like I love you.

Jem didn't have to even say the words anymore, even though Murphy liked to hear them, because he *knew* they were true.

Jem loved him, and he loved Jem.

Murphy reached over and flicked the light on.

Watched as Jem blinked as his eyes adjusted.

Tried not to panic as Jem stared at the gnome in front of him. No, the *gnomes*, plural.

Because once he'd started carving, the second gnome had blossomed so naturally, Murphy hadn't even realized it was happening until it was.

He'd told himself the whole time he'd been working on the piece that he could always separate them to be two individual statues. But then when he'd done the detail work on the hands, their fingers had ended up so intertwined he didn't have a hope or a prayer of breaking them up.

One of the gnomes was wearing a sweater and had Jem's easy smile. The other wore Murphy's signature plaid jacket and had a beard as thick as his own.

"You carved us together," Jem said, his tone full of wonder as he glanced back at Murphy.

Murphy tried to sound calm and collected and not like he was still freaking out a little bit that he'd done this. Yes, Jem loved him. Yes, Jem wanted to be with him. But this was a declaration of another kind entirely. Murphy knew it, he'd known it with each cut he'd made into the wood.

He just didn't know how Jem was going to feel about it.

"Yeah," Murphy said. He shrugged self-consciously. "I started your gnome, and he just didn't seem...right alone. The other one just *happened*, and then it felt so right, I kept going. I also decided, after the other night at the light tour, *not* to put you in a Condors jersey, because I wanted you to know that, no matter what, I don't see you as a football player, or Jeremiah Knight, I see you as *Jem*. But there is a little carved Condor, right on the hem of the sweater, because football is always gonna be a part of you." He took a deep breath. "If you hate it—"

But he didn't even get the rest of the sentence out. Jem threw his arms around him and hugged him tight and hard, Murphy staggering with the sudden movement. "God, I love it. I love every part of it. And you were right about the jersey," Jem said in a low, earnest voice. "It's perfect."

"Yeah?" Murphy's voice cracked on the word.

Jem pulled back, his face glowing with happiness and love. "*Yeah*. I mean, this is what I really wanted, even though I didn't tell you. You knew what I really felt, deep down, before I even did."

"I only knew what I wanted, more than anything, and I thought, stupidly maybe, that if I carved it, maybe it would come true."

"This was your wish, then?" Jem asked.

Murphy nodded. "Merry Christmas, Jem."

"I love you," Jem said.

And yeah, Murphy wasn't going to get over hearing that any time soon.

"I think I'm gonna die," Jem said over-dramatically. "I'm just gonna explode everywhere, and you're gonna have a heck of a cleanup after."

Murphy elbowed him in the side and Jem groaned again. That had been right in his stomach, and there was no question Murphy knew it, too. "You're gonna be fine. I told you to hold it on the appetizers. My mother likes to decorate with food. That doesn't mean *eat it all*."

"I wanted to make a good impression," Jem said mournfully, struggling into his jacket. He wasn't going to eat for a year. Next Christmas, he might be ready to sit down to another of Mrs. Clark's spreads. *Maybe*.

"Are you kidding me?" Murphy laughed. "My mother *loves* you. If she was any more pleased we're together, she'd be dragging us down to Town Hall today, holiday be damned." He flushed after his words, like he'd just realized what he'd said.

Jem laughed, too, both at his own ridiculousness, because of course the Clarks still liked him, and also because Murphy was so embarrassed he'd brought up marriage.

It was freaking adorable.

Jem hadn't known if he ever wanted to get married. He hadn't even thought about it, mostly because there hadn't ever been a person he'd wanted to be with for the rest of his life. But he could easily imagine spending every day after this with Murph.

He patted his inside pocket, the crinkle of the paper in it reassuring him that it was still there and present.

He hadn't given Murphy his own Christmas present yet, though he didn't think anything could ever equal the gnomes Murphy had carved for him.

"Fire's goin'," Murphy's dad said gruffly as they walked outside into the painfully crisp air. "Good thing the snow decided to let up."

"Just in time," Patricia said, walking up behind them and handing out big mugs, all decorated with gaudy snowmen or Santas or in Jem's case, an enormous gingerbread man who dominated the entire side.

He'd gone to so many of these Clark family bonfires as a kid. His parents had joined him too, sometimes, but often he'd just come himself, feeling as at-home with the Clarks as he had his own family.

Maybe that was why it had felt so right to slot in with Murphy like this, like this place had been waiting for him this whole time, and he hadn't even realized it until he was here. When he settled into it, it felt so right it was amazing he and Murphy hadn't been tucked up together like this the whole goddamn time.

Jem didn't think he could possibly put a single additional molecule of food or beverage into his body, but the mug felt warm against his palms, heating him through the same way Murphy's big body next to him did.

"This is nice," Joe Clark said in that gruff way, his gaze falling on Jem as he nodded approvingly.

Murphy tucked an arm around Jem, tugging him in closer as his dad tossed another few logs on the fire, the blaze lighting up the clearing they were standing in.

For a long time, they stood like that, the trees surrounding them, and the only sound penetrating the silence the crackling of the fire and Murphy's deep, contented breaths.

At some point, Joe and Patricia left, melting into the shadows with a wave and a quiet, "Merry Christmas."

Jem stared at the fire. Every Clark bonfire felt momentous, but this felt even more so, like his old life was crumbling to ash in front of him and in its place wasn't something he recognized, but he discovered he wasn't unhappy to discover what it looked like.

He'd never imagined being happy here in Christmas Falls, but then at the same time, he'd been happier and so much more content the last few weeks here than he'd ever imagined. Playing football in Charleston with Deacon and his teammates had been satisfying in a different kind of way. He certainly hadn't been unhappy doing that, but he'd known the whole time that wasn't a permanent situation.

This, on the other hand...

We love you too, brother, Deacon's voice added in his head. *And you won't ever be a stranger.*

He wouldn't be, and he didn't have any intention of permanently leaving Charleston.

But his future plans included not just the man next to him, but the town surrounding him.

"Hey," Jem said, turning to Murphy. "I thought...uh...I wanted to get you something for Christmas. Know you've never been big into gifts."

"It's something about all those people looking at me opening them," Murphy admitted. "But there's nobody here."

Jem reached into his pocket. "Nothing will ever top the gift you gave me this year. Seeing us together like that, and knowing you saw it in your mind, before we ever settled things between us..." He took a deep breath, his throat growing tight. Mrs. Lil had said he and Murphy had always been meant to be, and the more he settled into this relationship with him, the more obvious it was.

"I already got the best gift I could ever imagine this year. *You*," Murphy said, and Jem couldn't do anything else but lean in and kiss him, the envelope he'd pulled from his pocket crumpling between them.

The kiss was slow and sweet but drawn out, until Jem didn't want anything else but to take Murphy's hand and lead him to his own little cottage. Lose themselves in the big bed in his room.

But he needed to do this first.

Murphy hadn't pushed. He hadn't even asked. Of course, practically everyone else in town had, but Murphy hadn't. He'd just sat back and trusted that Jem would do what was right for him—and for them, together.

He handed Murphy the envelope.

"It's not much..." he said, trailing off. Feeling as awkward as he was sure Murphy had, right before he'd seen the gnomes he'd carved him. Truthfully, Jem wondered if this had been more a gift for *him*, but he didn't know how else to express to Murphy that while he'd been gone for too many years, that he was here *now*, and nothing was ever going to change that.

That Murphy wouldn't lose him again.

Murphy pulled the single sheet of paper out of the envelope and unfolded it, tilting it towards the light of the embers of the fire, finally beginning to burn out.

He didn't say anything for a long, painful moment.

Was he unhappy? Did he not understand?

Jem cleared his throat. "It's land," he explained. "I bought some land. I'm going to build a house here. And uh…I can't promise I won't ever visit Charleston again. I'm not going to sell that place. But this is where I'm gonna live. Once it's built, we can live there, in it, or you can stay here—"

Murphy turned to Jem, tears glittering in the corners of his eyes.

"You're moving here," he said breathlessly, like he could barely believe it.

"Yeah." Jem knew he should say something else, but what else to say? His throat felt tight. Saying *I love you*, even if it was for the millionth time, didn't feel like enough.

Maybe he should add something else, like, *I love you, and that's why, I can't live without you, not ever again.*

So he said it.

Watched as Murphy laughed and it was so easy, the easiest thing he'd ever done to pull the man he loved close and to kiss him again.

"Best Christmas present ever," Murphy said to him between kisses.

And Jem wasn't sure he could disagree—but he still had a few tricks up his sleeve.

Not for now, though

For now, this, with the fire burning in front of them, the trees sheltering them, and the sky and its blanket of stars above them, bells ringing out across the town as the clock hit midnight, was absolutely perfect.

Epilogue

Next year

"And now," Griff announced into the microphone, "I'm very pleased to introduce our judges for this year's pie bake-off. Of course, you know Mrs. Lil."

Jem watched from behind Griff as Mrs. Lil stepped forward, a tough but pleased smile on her face. He told himself he was not nervous—or uncertain—but it was still terrifying to stand up here, knowing what was about to happen.

Deacon gave him an encouraging nod, standing in the back of the audience, and it helped to know his best friend was supporting him, and not just in his own head this time around.

He and Murphy had met a few times over the summer—with way too many comments by Deacon about lumberjacks—but this winter was the first time Jem's best friend and his boyfriend had ever spent significant time together, and it wasn't surprising at all that they got along like a house on fire.

Or that Deacon had brought along his own partner for the festivities.

Finally, Jem thought.

"And also, our resident baker, Joel McArthur, of Ginger's Breads Bakery," Griff continued. "Last but not least, back by popular demand, Jeremiah Knight."

Jem waved to the audience and plucked his microphone out of Griff's hands. And Griff, who had become so much more relaxed and actually seemed to *enjoy* the festival these days, thanks to his own boyfriend, just smiled at him.

"Let's not fool around for a second," Jem said. "I wouldn't be anything without my faithful partner-in-crime. Murph, get up here."

Murphy flushed and reluctantly moved up on the stage, next to Jem, waving to the crowd.

Since he and Jem had started dating, Murph's gnomes had become even more in demand. He'd hired another employee, and now Tasha not only had two people to boss around—but a husband *and* a baby on the way.

"Let's start with the cream pies," Jem said to Murphy after Griff dismissed the panel to do their judging things.

Murphy held up two forks and gave him a look. "I thought we learned better than to do that last year. Didn't you *just* tell Mrs. Lil that you weren't an amateur anymore?"

"We'll never be amateurs," Jem said confidently, not quite feeling as sure of it as he sounded.

Murphy looked downright dubious. "Are you sure? You really want to start with the cream pies?"

"Oh, honey, I just love your cream so much," Jem teased, and Murphy went bright red, but there was absolutely a gleam of interest flashing in his dark eyes now.

"Honestly," Jem added, "never felt more sure of anything in my whole life."

Murphy raised an eyebrow. "That you want to start with the cream pies? Well, then, I guess you *aren't* an amateur anymore."

"I'm something," Jem muttered to himself as they walked down the table, set up with pie after pie. He had debated with himself all week about whether this was the right move, but after Deacon had gotten here, they'd discussed it, and Deacon had just said one thing that convinced him. *Do you love him?* he'd asked.

And yeah, he did.

More than anything.

Their house—because it had quickly become *their* house, the longer the construction crew worked on it—had finally been finished at the beginning of November, and Jem had been sure he knew what happiness was before he and Murphy had moved in, but this was a kind of bliss he'd never even believed existed.

"Alright," Murphy said, stopping at the last pie on the end. "Let's get this party started. This is a citrus cream." He handed Jem a fork and took his own, digging into the pie.

That was something else that had also convinced Jem this was the right thing to do.

In the last year, Murphy had come more out of his shell, not worrying so much about what people might think of their relationship. He'd learned that he was just as awesome as Jem was, and as their partnership had found an even footing, a back and forth, he'd fallen for his guy even harder.

"This is *really* good," Murphy said after a bite. "Come on, try it, Jem."

Jem scooped up some of the pale cream, and wished he'd left different instructions, because until he knew for sure that he wasn't the only one feeling this incredible bliss—and that he wasn't the only one angling to secure it, forever—everything was going to taste like ash in his mouth.

"Yeah, it's good," Jem said, even though he barely tasted it.

Or the next pie.

Or the next.

Finally, Murphy came to a stop in front of the fourth pie.

"This is the cranberry meringue from last year," Murphy said, and then his fork froze right above the pie.

Sitting on the crown on the meringue was the gleam of gold and silver—the ring Jem had personally had designed for Murphy. Two metals, twisted and curved together, echoing the two gnomes, holding hands, that sat in the front of their new home.

"What's this?" Murphy asked in a strangled voice.

"You know what it is," Jem said, discovering that his own was surprisingly steady.

Because yes, he loved Murphy, and he wanted this, more than anything else.

He snagged the ring off the top of the meringue and it was so easy to drop to one knee. "Murphy Clark, I love you. I've always loved you, but I came back last year, and I loved you, the same, but different. And this last year? It's been one of the best of my whole life, because we're finally together," he said, the echo of the wild screams and applause of the crowd barely making a dent. All he could see was Murphy and the wide, stunned look on his face. All he could hear were Murphy's short breaths.

Or maybe those were his own.

"Will you marry me?" Jem asked when Murphy still didn't say anything.

For one horrible, heart-stopping moment, he wondered if he'd made a mistake. If somehow he'd read Murphy wrong—but that felt impossible, because he knew him better than anyone he'd ever met. Including Deacon.

Then, Murphy slowly began to smile, and to Jem's shock, he pulled something out of his own pocket. A ring.

Oh God. Another ring.

"Guess you beat me to it," Murphy said, but he didn't sound disappointed. He sounded...well, he sounded just as happy as Jem felt.

"Guess I did."

"In case that wasn't clear, *yes*, yes I'll marry you. Happily. Gladly." Murph pulled him into an embrace and honestly, Jem had believed he was good before this moment.

But this one eclipsed all the others.

"Was gonna pop the question at the bench you kissed me at, that first time," Murphy said in a low voice as he slid the ring he'd purchased, solid and silver and heavy, onto Jem's finger. It felt right, and Jem realized he wouldn't have wanted this to turn out any other way. "But this was good too."

"Just felt like the perfect time to do it. At the place where I first knew I was falling for you," Jem said. His own ring fit perfectly onto Murphy's finger, and he sighed happily as he examined it.

"You like it?" Jem asked.

Murphy's eyes were shining as they lifted to his. "I love it," he said. "And I love you."

"Best Christmas present ever?" Jem teased. Thinking about their first Christmas last year, when he'd already been thinking about this and wanting it.

And how much more he'd wanted it now, a whole year later.

"Best everything, ever," Murphy declared, and Jem kissed him.

Because he couldn't deny, he felt the exact same way.

Want to read the Charleston Condors series?

You can check out the first three books in the series here.

Deacon & Grant's book, *The Play*, is out now!

INTERESTED IN READING MORE OF
BETH'S BOOKS?

CHECK OUT A FULL LIST OF TILES
BY SCANNING THE QR CODE
OR VISITING HER WEBSITE

WWW.BETHBOLDEN.COM/BOOKLIST

WANT TO FOLLOW BETH?

MAKE SURE YOU NEVER
MISS A RELEASE?

SCAN THE QR CODE BELOW
OR VISIT HER WEBSITE
FOR A SOCIAL MEDIA LIST,
NEWSLETTER SIGNUP,
AND SO MUCH MORE!

WWW.BETHBOLDEN.COM/ABOUT

9 781964 691183